THE PALE RIDER

JB TREPAGNIER

THE PALE RIDER

I wake up surrounded by death, and my memories are gone.

A man in a beige hazmat suit reaches his hand through the carnage. "Come with me if you want to live." I know I'm supposed to know that from somewhere, but I don't. I see the world outside me is not right. People either die or they are Rage Heads. Somehow, a virus got out that has turned people into red-eyed freaks who eat flesh. They are fast, their flesh is rotting off their bodies, and they have one goal—kill.

I don't know my mystery man in the hazmat suit, but he says I can trust him. He was at that lab looking for something. He claims not to have found it. He only found me. I see the way he looks at me when I ask what he was doing in that lab. I might feel safe with him, but he's lying to me. He knows everything about me, including the nickname people used to call me, but he tells me I ask too many questions. Maybe I'd be safer on my own.

The Pale Rider is Book 1 of End of Days. A post-

apocalyptic slow burn reverse harem romance. The harem will slowly grow as the books progress. The harem features the Four Horsemen of the Apocalypse.

To my Family

If you downloaded this book because you think you found my top-secret pen name, it wasn't me. It was other kids. I was dead at the time. Don't make Thanksgiving awkward.

END OF DAYS BOOK 1

I looked, and there before me was a pale horse! Its rider was named Death, and Hades was following close behind him. They were given power over a fourth of the earth to kill by sword, famine, and plague, and by the wild beasts of the earth.

ONE

I awoke to nothing but death. And a horrible smell. I didn't know where I was. I didn't know who I was. When my eyes fluttered open, I was dressed in a hospital gown in a white room. There was dust on the nightstand. I noticed that first. The place gave the appearance of some sort of long-term hospital room, but it didn't look like anyone had checked in on me for a while. And what was that smell?

I swung my legs off the bed and gently took the IV out of my hand. I didn't feel like I was in any type of pain to be needing drugs. Why was I here? Was I in some sort of coma? I tested my feet. I could stand. I was a little shaky, but I could walk. I made my way to the door. Where was everyone, and why was there dust in a hospital room? Could someone here tell me my name and why I was here? And for the love of God, *what was that smell?*

I managed to make it to the only door in the room. Locked. No one checked on me, but why did they lock me in this room? I pounded on the door and started screaming for someone, anyone to come to get me out of here. I didn't know how long I'd been in this room, but it was starting to feel tiny now that I knew they locked me in.

I pounded and pounded. My throat was parched like I hadn't drunk any water in months, but I kept screaming for someone to come get me. Was I alone in here? If this was a hospital, why wasn't there a nurse on duty?

Finally, I heard it. Footsteps in the hallway. I heard a muffled voice through the door.

"Stand away from the door!"

I stepped back, and whoever was on the other side started trying to kick the door in. I was so confused. What kind of hospital was I in, anyway? Was there something wrong with the key? Or was there something horrible going on beyond the other side of the door that they had to lock me in and not check on me for so long? I was getting bad vibes about the entire situation.

The door flew open, and I saw a man in a beige hazmat suit. *What the fuck was going on?* He held his hand out to me.

"Come with me if you want to live."

That line seemed so familiar, like I should know it, but at present, I didn't even know my own name or what I looked like. I could see on my arms that I was fond of tattoos at some point, and the ends of my hair were pink like I was a bit of a rebel, but I couldn't remember doing that. And if this guy really worked for some sort of search and rescue, why was he holding a baseball bat?

I shrunk back. I was noping all over this. I might not know much right now, but I knew not to trust strange men with their faces covered holding baseball bats. My eyes darted around the room, looking for a weapon that would beat a baseball bat or a place to hide. There wasn't even an empty tray in here I could beat this guy over the head with.

My fight-or-flight instincts were kicking in from somewhere unfamiliar. I had no idea what in my gut wanted me to fight this guy. He was much bigger than I was and may have known more about me than I did about myself. The logical part of my brain was saying to run and not look back, and my instincts were telling me to boot up and beat the shit out of this man.

He held his hands up in surrender, then offered me the baseball bat. I just started at it. It was baby blue, and there was something etched on the end. Why was this man offering me something to bash his head in with? What kind of day was it today that I wake up to crazy men in hazmat suits gifting me with baseball bats?

"Are you insane?" I hissed.

There was nothing I could say to him other than that, and if he was a crazy mother fucker, we should probably clear the air about that upfront.

He whipped his helmet off, and I was shocked at what I saw. He was actually good looking, and when a crazy guy is offering you a baseball bat when you don't even know your name, you probably shouldn't be checking him out. His hair was such a pale color of blond, it was almost white, and his eyes were a startling shade of gray. He looked like some sort of angel.

"What do you remember?" he demanded.

"Not a damned thing. The only thing I know is that an insane man is trying to give me a baseball bat in the middle of a hospital."

"Take the bat and see if you remember anything. It used to be yours."

I didn't take the bat. I wanted to know what the fuck was going on.

"Do you know me? What is my name, and what is going on in this hospital?"

He thrust the bat at me harder.

"Just take the bat."

"Not until you tell me my name."

He looked so irritated with me I wanted to take that bat and smack him upside the head with it. But then, I'd never find out my name.

"Your name is Ariel, but everyone calls you Speedy. Now, take the bat. We don't have a lot of time."

"Why does everyone call me Speedy?"

This big brute of a man just straight up grabbed my arm and yanked me out of the hospital room. Now I knew where the smell was coming from. I knew why there was dust in my room. All the staff was dead. It looked like something killed them and ate them in the hallway. The smell hit me even harder in the hall, and I dry heaved.

"Look at that, kitten. It's not pretty. See those teeth marks? The things that made them are swarming this building. I had to cut my way through them to find what I was after in this building. All I found was a girl without her memories in a hospital gown. Now, take the bat because you will need it to fight your way out of here. Even if you can't remember a fucking thing when you touch it, you need protection to make it out of here alive."

I might be confused, but I wasn't stupid. I was looking at an entire hallway of decaying, mangled corpses. I looked him right in the eye and grabbed that bat from him. I didn't know what was so important about that stupid, baby blue baseball bat, but when my hand wrapped around it, I felt this little surge, and I saw a flash.

I saw a crowd, and I felt a rush as they all cheered as I stepped up to the plate. I could see a field of women with tattoos like what I could see on my forearms, and they had colorful hair like the pink on my ends. I could hear a chant from the crowd. *Speedy, Speedy.* Was that me? The strange bat gifting man said people called me that. Why did people call me that? If I looked down, it was etched into the blue bat.

Just like the flash came into my mind, it was gone. I shook my head.

"What the fuck was that?"

"Did you remember anything?"

"A softball game."

The man shook his head.

"We're in the middle of nowhere surrounded by Rage Heads, and she remembers a fucking softball game."

"Well, you could give me a little more fucking help than handing me a baseball bat. I don't even know your name."

I heard this unreal wail come from down the hall. It didn't sound like it was alone, and it seemed like it was headed in my direction.

"Time to go, kitten, unless you want to get eaten."

I didn't know if I could trust this guy, and he was being pretty shifty about giving me information about myself and what he was doing in this hospital. I wasn't stupid, though. He was my best chance of getting out of this hospital alive. He had one chance to explain himself when we got out of here, and then I would ditch him and seek answers on my own.

I heard the pounding of footsteps. How many of those things were in here, and how did they move so fast? The man grabbed my hand and yanked me down the hall. Don't ask me where he got that fucking sword from.

"Aim for the head," he yelled as we tore ass down hallways littered with half-eaten bodies.

Good to know. I wished he would have given me a few more helpful tips before we took off running in this corpse infested hospital. I saw a flash of a softball game, but did I actually know how to wield this thing? I didn't even know my last name.

We almost made it out when the source of those wails popped out from behind a corner. There was no logical explanation for what was making those noises. They should have been dead and buried. Most of them had clothes that were hanging off their rotted frames. Their flesh was so nasty. It should have had maggots crawling out of it. The ones that still had eyes had this unnatural red tint to the whites of their eyes. I had no idea how they moved that fast, given the state of their decay.

There was way more of them than there were of us. There were worse things to have than a man with a sword who gifted you baseball bats and kept secrets when you were surrounded by walking corpses. I didn't know how I knew, but I would need both hands on that bat if I were supposed to be hitting these things in the head.

He was the only one who knew where we were going, but my survival instincts kicked in. I wrenched my hand out of his and took the bat in both hands. As soon as one of those things came near me, I swung as hard as I could. I guess I did use to be a softball player at some point because when my bat connected with this thing's head, it was like an overripe pumpkin. I was guessing it even sounded the same. I had to stop myself from vomiting.

I only had one goal here. Kill my way through these

things. But was it any better outside? If the hospital was like this, what was the rest of the world like?

It seemed like endless swinging and squelching noises before that wailing and hissing noise stopped. The man and I were standing among a pile of bodies, and there was black blood pooled at our feet. He just grinned at me.

"Not bad, kitten. Let's get as far away from here as possible."

"Not so fast. What is your name, and do you have a car?"

"My name is Aeron, and no one has cars anymore. There's no point. You can't get gas anywhere. I've got something better."

"Why should I trust you? You haven't given me much to go on."

"Because it's not just the Rage Heads you need to worry about. Humanity has gone to shit. If you want to stay safe out there, you need friends and supplies. I've got both."

"How do I know you're not part of the humanity that has gone to shit?"

"You don't. But you don't remember shit, and I have answers. You're just going to have to trust me, cupcake."

"Are you actually going to give me more answers than what you have?"

"I can help you get your memories back, and I can explain to you what is going on. But not here. It's not safe. I have a place we can go for the night, and there are separate beds in case you think I have any intention to rape you."

"I'll bash your fucking head in with this baseball bat if you tried."

"Keep Smurfette on you at all times."

"Smurfette?"

"That's what you used to call your bat."

I sighed and followed Aeron out of the hospital. The key to my past was in this grumpy ass, sword-wielding mother fucker who just showed up out of nowhere. I still didn't know if I would stay with him, but if I would find out who I was, I needed to leave with him and hear him out.

Two

"I'm not getting on that," I said, looking at Aeron's big fucking *horse*. That wasn't a normal horse. It wasn't white, but I couldn't describe its color except pale. It was way bigger than any horse should be, and I swear its eyes flashed red at me.

"Meremoth is a champion stallion, and he obeys me. You just need to sit up there while I control him. You aren't scared of a horse after you just killed all those Rage Heads, are you?"

"Why is he so big, and why did his eyes flash red like that?"

"He's big because all horses of his breed are that size. It was just a trick of the light. As you can see, Meremoth has perfectly normal eyes."

"You're telling me people use horses instead of cars now?"

He just shrugged.

"No, most people aren't lucky enough to have a horse and go on foot. I could always ride him and make your ungrateful ass walk all ten miles home."

"Has anyone ever told you that you are a huge asshole?"

"Well, you're being a spoiled brat. It's the end of the world. You need to be a little more grateful when people are offering to share their shit with you because there are some people out there who would just as well cook you and eat your flesh."

"Well, you haven't exactly told me what's going on and why we got attacked by corpses."

"Look at your surroundings, kitten. What do you think is going on?"

I looked past the horse. The sky wasn't blue. It was some sickly orange color. Any grass I could see was dead. There were cars just abandoned, some on the sidewalk, some on the road and parking lot. Some of them, I could see dead bodies inside, and some had the doors open like someone had looted the car to see what was inside.

"How did this happen?"

"Not here. It's not safe. Now, will you get on my fucking horse so we can get home sooner, or do you want to risk hoofing it on foot?"

"Sorry. I'll get on the horse, but do you think you could be a bit more patient? I don't even know my last name, much less what's going on."

Aeron ran his fingers through his white hair.

"This sure would be easier if you remembered," he muttered.

The horse was so huge, I couldn't even imagine how I was supposed to get myself in the saddle. I couldn't reach it.

"A little help?" I asked Aeron.

This guy right here. He picked me up and practically threw me in the saddle. If I hadn't grabbed the pommel, I would have flown completely over this fucking horse. He didn't even give me a chance to settle before he heaved himself after me.

Oh. Were we going to sit like this? I didn't even know this guy, and his crotch was pressed right up against my ass. He held the reins in one hand and wrapped his other arm around my waist. This was a little... intimate considering I didn't know his last name or mine, and he was kind of an asshole.

I threw the kind of out the window and upgraded him to total asshole when he kicked his horse, and the thing started running so fast, I was sure I would fall off. I shrieked and clutched the pommel. Aeron tightened his hold around my waist.

"Calm down. We'll slow down when we are less exposed. Don't draw attention to us, or you'll bring a swarm on us, or worse, stupid humans still using guns."

"Why wouldn't you want a gun during the end of the world?"

"Rage Heads are drawn by sound and smell. A gun will draw every Rage Head within a fifteen-mile radius to you. Most smart people don't use them anymore and have learned to hunt with bows."

"Will you teach me?"

I was starting to think I would stay with Aeron long enough to survive on my own and find some place to hunker down. Why did he have my baseball bat from who knew how long ago and know what I called it? He said he was at that hospital looking for something and heard me pounding. I was guessing he didn't find it and found me instead.

If he wasn't looking for me, how did he know so much about me, and where did he get that bat? Something wasn't sitting right with the mysterious Aeron and me.

I'd hear him out, but depending on what he said, I may or may not stay with him. He was kind of a grumpy fuck.

THREE

The crazy asshole driving the horse did eventually slow down when we got to narrow roads with a lot of tree cover. Where were we anyway? I didn't recognize any of this landscape, and I wasn't getting any flashes like when I touched the bat.

"Aeron? Where exactly are we?"

"Waterville, Washington. It's pretty remote. We won't be staying. We'll be meeting someone in Mexico."

"Who said I was staying with you?"

"I did. I found you, I rescued you, and I'm claiming you. You're coming to D.C. with me."

"Excuse me? You can't claim me if I don't want to be claimed."

"Don't be stupid. I can't protect you if I don't claim you. Important things are waiting in D.C. We have to make pit stops in Mexico and Florida to pick people up. Then, we are going to Washington D.C. to stop the end of the world."

"Well, don't you just think you've got the biggest balls in the world?"

"I do. I've also got a plan that will work. I'm not asking you to like me, cupcake. I'm asking you to do the smart thing and help us."

"How exactly am I supposed to help you with that?"

"Just trust me. Now be quiet. Scooter's gang patrols these woods. They are trigger happy and cannibals. I have no desire to be eaten alive by Rage Heads or a bunch of human jackasses. Just stay silent for the next two miles. You'll get your answers when I get home."

I zipped my mouth, but I was dying to know what exactly happened that corpses *and* humans were eating people. And what the fuck happened to me that I slept through it and couldn't remember my name? How long had I been in that hospital, anyway? Why did this blue baseball bat trigger memories for me?

I kept my mouth shut until Aeron pulled the horse up to what looked like a remote cabin. Was this what the world had come to? The cottage had high barbed wire and a trench with wood spikes out front. There was a wriggling corpse impaled on a pike as Aeron led the horse through the front gate.

It was a small cabin made out of logs. I was a little shocked when he helped me off the horse, we went inside, and he pulled cold water out of the refrigerator.

"I'm not an expert on the end of the world, but I thought everyone lost power. The hospital must have had backup generators."

"That's what this place has. I only run it for the fridge and the stove. I siphon gas out of cars to run it. I was lucky to find this place."

"You don't live here?"

Aeron just scoffed.

"Hardly."

"Then, why were you here, and what were you looking for at that hospital?"

"First of all, it wasn't a hospital. It was a research facility. I thought part of my plan was there, but it was incomplete."

"Do you know why I was at that research facility? Am I from here?"

"You are from California. Should I call you Ariel or Speedy?"

"I don't know. I didn't know either name until you told me. How do you know all this stuff about me if you were looking for something else at that research facility?"

"Here's the thing, Speedy. I can't give you all your memories back at once without hurting you. I can tell you all about the end of the world, but as for your past, we will have to do that in bits and pieces. I'm doing this because it can seriously hurt you if we do it the other way."

"Fair enough. How did all *this* happen?"

"Pure evil."

If those were the kinds of answers he would give me, then what was I staying here for? He saw the look I was giving him. He knew I was about to grab that blue baseball bat and hightail it out of this cabin.

"Wait. I wasn't finished. This started on purpose. They created those Rage Heads. A company named Armilus started creating nutritional supplements. They got a patent for a supplement kind of like fluoride to add to water that was supposed to help strengthen bones. It was tasteless, and the clinical trials showed an eighty percent reversal of osteoporosis and helped with arthritis pain."

Armilus. That named sounded like I should know it,

but I wasn't getting any flashes. Did I know it before I lost my memories?

"Why does the name Armilus seem so familiar?"

Aeron narrowed his eyes at me like he desperately wanted me to remember something.

"Armilus is a figure from Jewish lore. He's the son of Satan."

"Am I Jewish? Why would I know that? And if there was a company peddling supplements named after the son of Satan, why didn't anyone shut that shit down?"

"There were many people that knew what the company was named after and didn't trust the company. They were legitimate at first. The product was helping people, and they were getting contracts all over the world. It was getting added to bottled water all over the place and seemed harmless for years."

"So, how did it go from harmless to the apocalypse?"

"They started seeking contracts with local municipalities to have it added to the water supply. By then, even the people who spoke against them couldn't find a reason to distrust them. They started thinking they picked a name for the company, not researching and genuinely knowing what it meant. That happens sometimes, but not in this case.

"The product started cropping up in minor cities first, then larger. Still, it was harmless, and there wasn't much reason to distrust the water. It was a bait and switch. Sometime around 2034, Armilus started shipping the altered product out to be put into the water supply."

I looked down at the cold bottle of water I had been chugging since my throat was so parched. My hand started shaking. Did he just dose me with Satan tainted water?

"What did you just give me to drink?"

"Water," Aeron said, grinning at me like he didn't just tell me water turned people into cannibal corpses. "Not all bottled water companies used the supplement. The ones that didn't advertised pretty heavily, and they had a following. Well water is still safe. The cities that use well water didn't use the supplement. Since you don't know, today is June 19, 2044. The places that have generators and running water have safe water.

"Armilus was a billion-dollar corporation with a huge marketing department, but it was like they just disappeared off the planet when people started getting sick. To this day, most people don't know it was them that started all of this."

"And how do you know? I agree, naming your company after the son of Satan puts a huge target on your back, but if no one else knows, how does a guy living in a cabin in the middle of nowhere know?"

Aeron's silver eyes caught the light, and I swear, it was like the horse. They looked like they were glowing white for a moment. Who the fuck was this guy, anyway?

"Trust me, I know, Speedy. I know who started this, and I know how to end it. I know you don't remember shit, but know this. Me and the people we will meet along the way are the only people you can trust in all of this."

Easy for him to say. I still didn't know his last name, and he could be some post-apocalyptic conspiracy theory nut that sat around with a tinfoil hat on his head when he wasn't handing out blue baseball bats to people without their memories.

"Who *are* you?" I asked. "What were you really doing at that hospital?"

"You're not ready for any of that, Speedy. In time. I

still haven't filled you in on everything that has happened."

There was more? I mean, there were walking corpses with red eyes that moved like lightning and ate people. I got the memo. Things went to shit.

"So, tell me."

"Some people were immune to the mutation that the supplement caused. We've narrowed it down to blood type. The only people who drank the water and didn't turn are AB negative. You would be AB negative if you wanted to know. The supplement caused a mutation in the brain and blood. It always started with broken blood vessels in the eyes and ended with extreme rage.

"At first, they tried to sedate them. Jails and institutions started filling up with violent people. No one knew what was wrong. The government was telling everyone it was this new street drug called Halo, but people knew that was wrong. It was affecting people with no history of drug use. People in nursing homes were becoming violent, and so were small children."

"How did it go from violent to what I saw at that clinic?"

"I'm getting there. The mutation had a progression. It started with the whites of the eyes. The second stage was irrational violence that no sedation could touch. No one knew it would eventually become fatal or what would happen after.

"It happened almost simultaneously. The first time anyone realized what a mess this would be was when the cops responded to a case in New Orleans, and a man in a mental institution died. A man had gone totally crazy on Bourbon street and was beating up tourists. Understand, back then, some people believed the government that these people were just high on drugs.

"This man was in such a rage, and he couldn't be captured and brought in. The tasers did nothing to him. He beat two cops almost to death before they shot him in the chest. Almost at the exact same time, all the way across the world, a young man at a mental institution started pouring blood from his eyes, nose, and mouth. No one realized this, but they died almost at the same time, and they rose almost at the same time."

"Excuse me, rose? You are talking about a mutation caused by a company named after the son of Satan and people rising from the dead? I might not know what day of the week it is, but that sounds ridiculous."

Aeron sighed and rubbed his temples.

"I need you to believe this now because it only gets worse from here. I need you on our side, Speedy. I really wish you had woken up with your memories."

I had so many questions, and I didn't know where to start. I couldn't exactly get all offended he was trying to tell me people rose from the dead when I just crushed the head of walking corpses with a baseball bat, but if I was just some random girl he found when he was looking for something at the facility, how did he know so much about me and why did he want me to remember so badly? The only way I would find out was to let him keep talking.

I held up my hand.

"Truce. Finish your story, and I'll try not to interrupt unless I have to."

"No. Stop me if you have questions. Maybe it will jog a memory loose. Ask me as many questions as you want because you need to understand this."

"Fair enough. So, two people rose from the dead. What happened?"

"One man took five bullets to the chest, and the other was legally pronounced dead by the facility trying to save his life. Before they could even move the body, it jumped up and took a bite out of the nearest living person. No one knew this at the time, but the only way to kill them is to kill the brain, and the AB negative immunity to the water doesn't hold if you get bitten by one of them."

"How does that work? If certain blood types are immune, why does that change if you get bitten?"

"My team has studied this extensively. I told you, we know what's going on. Once you are exposed, it's a constant mutation. We caught a Rage Head alive and studied it. We tested its blood daily, and it was never the same. We think it constantly mutates to keep the corpse alive. When the body dies, another mutation happens that AB negative blood types don't have an immunity to."

"So, don't let one of those things bite me. Got it."

Aeron opened his mouth to say something, then stopped himself. There was something he would tell me and stopped himself.

"Not to mention getting a hunk of your flesh torn off with human teeth hurts like a mother fuck. Like I said, keep that bat on you at all times and don't let them get close to you."

"You would say something else, Aeron. Tell me."

"Not quite yet. I need to fill you in on everything you missed. The government tried to keep this under wraps and not let people know it was happening, but a man literally rose from the dead in the middle of a street of tourists in Bourbon street. As you can imagine, not everyone was running for their lives as a dead man started eating tourists and cops. There's always that one asshole sitting there filming everything on their cell phone."

"And the asshole sitting there pointing their cell phone at the scene instead of running didn't get eaten?"

"They never do, Speedy. They never do. The tourists that lived went home and were spreading stories while the government tried to do damage control. The president went on live television to debunk the story. Other countries were having the exact same issue, and they were following suit. They were all trying to deny the dead were rising to keep people from panicking.

"It would have worked, but more than one person was recording in New Orleans that day. The more the various governments tried to deny what was going on, the more upset they got. They started uploading their footage to social media. By the time anyone important realized it was up, it had already gone viral."

"Let me guess. They kept flagging the videos and taking them down, but they kept re-uploading them, and everyone got pissed off at the government."

"Exactly. It just got worse when people started running out of food. You were either in the process of mutating, or you were immune and trying to stay safe. No one could go to the grocery store anymore because they weren't being staffed. There was mass looting and stealing from neighbors. Cities became ghost towns, and food became scarce. People who were mad at the government for lying about the dead were now angry at them for not fixing this and getting them food.

"That was when war broke out. Some thought their governments would come through and fix all of this and those that wanted an entire regime change. Instead of focusing on finding some sort of cure and helping each other stay safe from the Rage Heads, they were killing each other."

"This sounds familiar, but I don't remember any of it."

"Let me finish, and all of it will sound familiar. After the fighting stopped, people tried to seize power. The countries you remember are gone. Mexico and Canada are now part of the United States and run by a dictator. Most of Europe is all one country and run by one man. It's the same with the Eastern countries. All of these men have found a way to communicate in these end times, and they run things together. My intel says Isaiah Nahum, the man who is now the president of the United States is calling all the shots around the world. Is that triggering any memories?"

"Should it?"

Really, should it? Was I somehow a part of all of this? Why couldn't he just tell me the truth?

"In time. Does any of this sound familiar to you?"

"Well, you have all the ingredients for the end of the world. Pestilence, famine, war, and conquest. How exactly do you plan to end all that by going to Washington, D.C.?"

Aeron just gave me this wicked grin.

"Because I have all the ingredients to stop all that."

"How, when you didn't find what you were looking for at that clinic?"

"Think, Speedy. Where is it written that the world will end with pestilence, famine, war, and conquest?"

"Every movie about the end of the world?"

"Think older."

My body broke into goosebumps, and I got another flash. I saw my tattooed arms on a table reading a book.

No, I was reading specific passages in the bible, and I was studying it hard.

"A company named after the son of Satan and the Book of Revelations? How are you going to stop something biblical?"

"We will kill the President of the United States."

FOUR

Was my life before this as fucked up as before I woke up in that clinic? I mean, I had pink hair, Alice in Wonderland tattoos all over my arms, and I named a blue baseball bat Smurfette. I still had no idea why everyone called me Speedy, but it had to be a lot more reasonable than killing the president for biblical reasons for some end of the world conspiracy theory.

"Are you some whack job, Aeron? How is killing the President of the United States going to stop any of this?"

"Remember Armilus, Speedy? Care to guess who was secretly the majority shareholder in that company? Isaiah Nahum. They planned all this."

"You've told me stories. Do you actually have any proof?"

Aeron bolted to his feet.

"Stay here."

When he came back out, he had a rucksack with him. I watched him pull a laptop out. I would have thought laptops would be obsolete, considering almost nothing had power unless there were backup generators. He powered it on and opened a file. A photo of a man pulled up. He was totally bald with bright blue eyes. There was something off about him.

"This is Isaiah. He didn't use to be bald. He started shaving his head after he inserted himself as president."

"He looks like an asshole. He looks like the kind of guy who would try to run a country during the end of the world, but how is killing him going to stop anything?"

Aeron looked totally irritated with me. Was this supposed to trigger some sort of memory? I was pretty sure I'd never met that guy before, but if he said I had, was I an awful person, and that was why I was in that clinic?

"Was I a wicked person, Aeron? Did you show me this photo because I knew this man and helped him? Do you want to get us together so you can kill us both?"

Aeron finally gave me this soft look like he might be a friendly person underneath all the gruff.

"You know him in a way, but you aren't like him. You are nothing like him. We don't plan on killing you. I really do wish you remembered something."

"Why can't you just tell me about myself? What's the big deal about telling me?"

"Because of the way your memories were taken, Speedy. If I trigger them in the wrong way, you will go insane."

Way to totally shit in my memory loss cornflakes. I guess I would have to deal with not knowing a damned thing about myself until it slowly came back to me. I guess I was just going to have to deal with it because I certainly didn't want to lose my mind when the apocalypse was going on.

"Can you at least tell me why they call me Speedy, and I have a blue bat named Smurfette?"

I couldn't believe it, but he actually smiled at me. I didn't think this grumpy fuck was actually capable of it.

"Yes, I can. When you were in college, you played in a roller derby league. In 2028, it came in fashion for girls who were retiring from roller derby to start a fastpitch softball team. It really caught on. All the fans who enjoyed rooting for them came out to watch the games. You played shortstop, and they called you Speedy when you were playing roller derby too because you've always been fast. I've never seen you play, but I heard you were a hell of a softball player."

"I played roller derby and softball?"

"Yes, and roller derby is pretty cutthroat. I knew when I handed you that bat, you'd be able to kill anything that came at you with it, even if it didn't trigger any memories."

"*How* did you get my old softball bat? You said you were looking for something at that clinic. If you weren't looking for me, why did you have my bat and know so much about me?"

"I've got clothes from your apartment too, but that's all I can tell you for now."

I was about to fire off a million questions, but my stomach twisted in on itself and let out this tremendous growl. I realized how hungry I was. When was the last time I ate real food, anyway?

Aeron bolted to his feet.

"Storytime is over. You need to eat something. I've still got deer I hunted in the freezer, and this cabin had a veggie plot when I found it. It was overrun with weeds, but I cleared it out, and I've got fresh veggies to feed you."

He dug around in his rucksack and pulled out a little baggy. He tossed it at me and headed to the kitchen.

"That's some deer jerky I made. Chew on that while I cook. We aren't always going to have the luxury of me finding a place like this. We may have to sleep in the woods or a place with no power. I lucked out finding this place."

I followed him into the kitchen, chewing on the deer jerky. It tasted good, and I was so hungry, I would have eaten just about anything right now.

"Did you put the castle fortifications outside, or did someone else?"

"That was here when I found the place."

I wasn't sure I wanted to know the answer to this, but I asked anyway. I had to know who I agreed to travel with.

"What happened to the previous owners?"

"Someone must have gotten bitten on a supply run for gas for the generator. When I found this place, the generator was all gassed up, and there were three eaten corpses and a Rage Head looking for a meal. I gave him mercy and killed him. I buried them out back."

I just had this feeling he wasn't lying about that. He wanted to kill the president, but he didn't kill people for supplies. And he was cooking deer meat, so he wasn't a cannibal.

I wasn't sure if I was on board for killing the President of the United States, but he seemed handy to have around during the apocalypse. And he knew more about me than I knew about myself. I decided I would follow him to Washington, D.C.

Five

Aeron was such a strange man. I knew why he couldn't talk about my past, but I tried to get him to talk about his as we ate, and he answered me in grunts. He even told me he didn't have one when I asked him his last name. I tried to ask him more about the people we would be meeting. He said there were three, and they were all specialists in their field. They worked together at first, getting a picture of all of this, then they scattered. He was in Washington, one was in Mexico, one was in Florida, and the other was in D.C. monitoring the president.

He said he had already alerted them he found me and would come to them, but that made little sense. He never left my side since he kicked my door down, and I didn't see him contact anyone. Plus, I was pretty sure cell phones didn't work anymore, and that laptop of his didn't get Wi-Fi. He refused to answer when I asked how.

I was still asking questions when he started clearing plates away. He finally turned to me.

"This place still has running water. Why don't you go take a shower and change into some real clothes? I'm sure you're tired of that hospital gown."

I hadn't even thought about the fact that my ass had been hanging out of this gown this entire time. Did I get embarrassed about that kind of stuff before? I turned on my heels to find the bathroom with my bare butt on full display, and I didn't care at all. Should I? Right now, I didn't give a fuck.

Aeron must have cleaned up this place when he found it because I didn't see a sign anyone had been eaten here. The bathroom was cozy but neat. I finally got to see what I looked like. I knew my hair was blonde with pink ends, and I had full Alice in Wonderland sleeves tattooed on both arms, but I also had blue eyes, and I wasn't half bad looking.

When I got the gown off, I found more tattoos. I must have been a big reader because they were all based on fairy tales. I had a scene from The Little Mermaid on one thigh and Little Red Riding Hood on the other. They were all pretty well done. I guess that was one bright side to this. I didn't know a single thing about my past, but at least I didn't have shitty tattoos.

The water was cold, but it would be way too much to ask to have a hot shower considering everything that was going on. I washed my hair and body with a green bar of soap that I was pretty sure was Irish Spring. Soap was probably a huge luxury right now, and I was grateful for anything to wash with. I didn't know how long I'd been in that hospital, but at most, I'd probably gotten a sponge bath, and that was it.

The idea of just sponge baths for who knew how long

made this shower a precious thing. And who knew the next time I would get one. I hadn't been awake for that long, but I wasn't taking anything for granted. Even the man who cooked me dinner and was sharing all this with me. He might be secretive and grumpy, but he could have left me there to starve. I knew that might change. I wasn't sure I altogether trusted him just yet, but I was happy to have a hot meal and a place to sleep tonight. And he gave me a little about my past and explained what was going on with the world.

I turned off the water and wrapped a towel around myself. When I stepped outside, Aeron had left another rucksack by the door. I peered inside, and there were girl clothes in there. He mentioned something about going to my old apartment, and I had fifty million questions about that.

It had to mean something. I meant something. He said I wasn't bad, but I was involved in this somehow. Someone put me in that remote research facility, and I was in a coma for a reason. These four people wanted me in D.C. for something more than just killing the president. Aeron would not tell me until I had my memories back, and who knew when that would happen?

I wandered around the cabin until I found a bedroom that looked like Aeron wasn't sleeping in. I dumped the clothes on the bed. What kind of person was I? I liked tattoos, but what kind of clothes did I like? I pawed through them to find out.

Lacy lingerie and leather if these clothes were any indication. Was there anything to sleep in? I just got the feeling I was the type of person who slept naked before, but during these times, that probably wasn't safe anymore. You couldn't have that much exposed flesh if a Rage Head broke into the house, and if humans broke in, you were just asking to get raped. Would I even have pajamas at my old apartment?

I pulled a lacy pair of boy shorts on and found some yoga pants. There were some T-shirts in there, but I had apparently altered them. Most of them were band T-shirts like I used to go to a lot of concerts. I'd cut the neck out of the shirts and altered the sleeve, so all the shirts ended up being off the shoulder.

I yanked a shirt over my head, and when it settled, I broke into goosebumps and got a flash. I was with a girl at a concert. It was the band on my T-shirt. I knew the girl. We were friends. Everyone called her Pokey, and I knew her from roller derby and softball. She played first base, and we worked well together as a team with me playing shortstop.

We loved this band. This was our fourth time seeing them. We saw them every time they came to California. Los Angeles. I lived in Los Angeles before. What was I doing in Washington State?

Just like that, the memory stopped. I went barging out of the bedroom to find Aeron. Maybe if I told him what I remembered, he'd tell me more about myself. I needed to know. It was killing me, not remembering anything. The lights outside of my bedroom were out.

Aeron's bedroom door was shut, and his light was out. I realized he was probably sleeping. I knew he would be happy I remembered something, but he was also a grumpy fuck, and I didn't know how he felt about his beauty sleep. I wasn't about to go barging in his bedroom and find out either. What if he slept naked too? He was hot, and there was a part of me that wouldn't mind getting a peek, but what if he was one of those prudish people that didn't enjoy showing off?

I needed this. I needed Aeron for now. I would not risk it. I turned and went back to my bedroom to sleep.

Six

I'm five years old. I'm at a sterile white facility. I don't want to be there. Two people in lab coats are restraining me. A man is walking away from me, but I don't want him to leave. All I can see is his back. He's dressed in an expensive suit, and his shoes are just so shiny.

"Don't leave me here!" I shriek.

He doesn't turn back. I love this man, but it's like he doesn't love me, or he wouldn't leave me or would come back and explain to me why I had to stay here.

"Please, come back!"

The men restraining me start to pull me towards a set of white doors. I fight. Pain is behind those doors. I've been before, and I don't want to go back. I will fight to the death to not have to go back. I bite the man closest to me, but he's so much bigger than I am.

He yanks his arm away from me and curses. He backhands my tiny face, and I crumple to the floor. The other man just leaves me there while I sob.

"Watch it. You know we are not to leave marks on this one."

"Then, drug her. He could at least give us the courtesy of giving this brat something to calm her down before he brings her here. I'm tired of her fighting us."

"This brat pays our salary, and he said no marks. Deal with it."

"Then, drug her. If she bites me again, I will hurt her bad."

I feel the pinch of the needle as it goes into my thigh. I'm still whimpering from the throbbing in my cheek as my vision goes black. I tell myself before I passed out that one day, I will be big enough to fight them off so they can't do this to me again.

I bolted to a sitting position with tears streaming down my face and phantom pain in my cheek. Was that a nightmare, or did that really happen to me? Who was that man, and why was he paying people to hurt me? Did it have anything to do with the research facility I ended up in?

I had no idea what time it was, but there was no way I was going back to sleep now. I padded into the living room, and Aeron was already awake. He was in the kitchen cooking eggs. I peered over his shoulder.

"The eggs are powdered. It's not fancy, but it's hot. I'll be using the last of the deer. I have turned the rest into jerky. We'll be setting out tomorrow. We should make a supply run later today. Do you think you can handle yourself if I take you to town? It's pretty basic. Stay quiet and bash the head of anything that comes close to you."

"Yeah, I think I can manage that. I don't think I'm a picky eater. I don't care if the eggs are powdered. I'm sure it'll taste great. We won't have that luxury when we leave here, right?"

"Correct."

"Need any help? I feel bad you are doing all this work, and I'm not helping at all."

"The only thing you need to worry about right now is staying alive and getting your memories back."

"Was I at another research facility when I was a child?"

"Why do you ask that?"

"I had a nightmare. A man dropped me off at a scary hospital. I didn't want to be there, and they were hurting me. He left me anyway and didn't look back. I tried to fight, and one man straight-up hit me."

"That was a memory, not a nightmare, Speedy. Don't fight it when they come. Not all of your memories are happy softball games."

"Why was I at a research facility as a child, then again as an adult?"

"All I can tell you was that your father was an asshole. I'm sure you gathered that from your dream."

"But I could feel that I loved him from the dream. I wanted him to come back and save me. Why would I love him if he did that to me?"

"Everyone wants to love their father no matter how much of a dick they are."

I asked, even though I knew I would probably get a grunt in return.

"What about you? Do you love your father?"

Aeron grunted, and I didn't think he would answer.

"You could say they programmed me to love my father no matter what he does or doesn't do."

"Did your father do anything as bad as mine did?"

Aeron got up and stormed out the room.

"Yeah, he created me," he snapped on the way out.

What did that even mean? I knew why Aeron

couldn't tell me more about my past, but why was he so secretive about his? There wasn't much we could talk about right now. It wasn't like I could ignore him and binge watch TV. I clearly enjoyed reading based on my tattoos, but I had nothing to read on, and the previous inhabitants of this cabin didn't leave a single book behind.

I wasn't taking this. If he wanted this to work, he would have to be honest with me. How could I trust him that he was telling the truth about all of this if he couldn't even tell me about himself?

I followed him out of the room. He slammed his bedroom door in my face, and I just kicked it right open. He spun around panting when he realized I was in his private space.

"Get out!" he roared.

"No!" I yelled. "You ask me to trust you with your crazy tale. You tell me you have the solution to all of this and can end it. How am I supposed to believe anything you say when anytime I ask you about yourself, you just grunt at me?"

"Believe me, Ariel, if you think the story I told you is ridiculous, you will think my past is totally insane until you get your memories back! Be patient!"

"You won't even tell me your last name! You lied and told me you didn't have one!"

"That's because I don't!" he yelled. "None of the four people you will meet have them, so don't bother asking us."

"Are you related?"

"In a way. We have the same father."

"And he didn't give you his last name?"

"He doesn't have one either."

Aeron had this slight accent that I couldn't place. Was

that common where he was from? Since he was finally answering questions a bit, I decided just to ask.

"Where are you from, Aeron?"

His mood instantly changed. He got this smirk on his face and pointed to the sky.

"Up north, you could say."

"Canadians have last names, Aeron."

Aeron fell out laughing. He had to sit down, and he was clutching his side as tears ran down his face, he was laughing so hard.

"I will tell my brothers you think we're Canadians."

"The North Pole?"

Aeron just sat there, giggling.

"If you mean further north than the North Pole, I will not believe you if you say you're an alien."

Aeron lost it again.

"Humans are so strange," he wheezed.

"Wait, you're seriously claiming to be an alien?"

"I'm not an alien, Ariel."

"Then why won't you tell me where you are from?"

"Because you'd leave. You need more of your memories back before you learn more about me, or you'll run."

"What if I run because you are keeping secrets?"

Aeron just shrugged.

"Ask me something that isn't my last name or where I'm from, and I'll answer it if I can."

I crossed my arms and glared at him. What was so bad about his past that I would run? And how was it weirder than me thinking he was an alien? I just needed to be patient. He promised me answers, just not yet. I would eventually get them. I may get tired and leave before I got them, but for now, I could wait.

"Favorite food. Go."

"Chinese food for the meal, Indian food for the dessert."

"How do you manage that without going to two restaurants?"

"Magic."

"What's my favorite food?" I asked.

"Cheetos. It's always been Cheetos."

How did he know that? Would he even tell me if I asked? I might as well try since he was finally not grunting at me.

"How do you know all this about me? Have we met before, and I don't remember?"

"No, Ariel. You've never met us before. But you've been on our radar for a very long time."

"Okay, then. Tell me about your team. You said you all had a specialty. Can you tell me about that? How exactly are the four of you experts in stopping the end of the world?"

Aeron puffed his chest out and got a little swagger in his step as he walked over to the bed. He flopped on his back and stuck his hands behind his head.

"We are *exactly* who you want on your side at the end of the world. Leif specializes in diseases. Asher is a master of justice. Dice can come up with any battle strategy. As I said, we can do this."

"What's your specialty?" I asked, crossing my arms.

Aeron's mood totally darkened. He hopped off the bed and stalked out the room.

"The only thing I'm good at is death. Question time is over."

I sighed. At least I got a little out of him.

SEVEN

Almost as soon as this grumpy fuck stormed out the bedroom, he just came stomping back in. I went to follow him and ran straight into his hard chest and ended up on my ass. Did I mention he was huge? He didn't even apologize or help me to my feet. He just glared down at me.

"Get dressed. We need to go on a supply run, and since you've never been on one before, it will take longer than usual. We have to be back before it gets dark and we have to avoid Scooter's gang. They'd love to get their hands on a pretty girl. I don't think I need to graphically explain to you what that means. Go put some clothes on, Speedy."

Asshole. I shoved him out of the way as I made my way back to my bedroom. If I didn't need him for now, I would have kicked him straight in the balls. I dug through the clothes in the rucksack. I would say this for myself before I lost my memories. I had good taste in clothes. I pulled a pair of well-worn leather trousers out that felt like butter and fit me like a second skin. I pulled a shirt on and grabbed Smurfette from the side of the bed. I didn't remember much, but I felt a lot safer with that baby blue bat resting on the pillow next to me while I slept.

I slung the bat over my shoulder and went back into the living room. Aeron scanned me from head to toe with this look on his face that he quickly hid. He threw an empty rucksack at me that would have hit me in the face if I hadn't caught it. Dick.

"Canned goods and non-perishables only. If you see bottled water, don't put it in your bag until you've shown it to me, and I can verify it's safe. If we hit up a store with a pharmacy attached, it'll probably already be raided, but we still need to go through it. Most likely, they've taken anything that gets you high, but we might luck out and find antibiotics. If you find over-the-counter pain meds, grab them. Those are solid gold. Get in, get out, stay quiet, and try not to be seen. There will probably be Rage Heads loitering about. Kill them as quietly as you can. The noise you hear them make in the hospital is how they call each other. They hunt in herds."

"Got it."

Aeron just sniffed.

"I highly doubt it. Just stay close to me until we've cleared the store and don't wander."

This asshole right here. I waited while he saddled that creepy horse, and I knew I didn't imagine it the other day when its eyes flashed red. I swear that thing's eyes flashed red again, and it *winked* at me. He came at me like he would throw me on top like last time.

"Can you put me up there like I'm a human and not a sack of potatoes this time?"

Aeron just grunted at me again. Of course, the one man I'm stuck with during the apocalypse speaks in grunts and happens to be a dick. But at least I didn't have to desperately grab for something as I went flying over that beast. He was much more gentle as he put me on the back of the horse this time.

Aeron climbed on behind me, and I so shouldn't be thinking about what his muscular chest felt like pressed against my back when he was such a douche. Did I date total assholes before I lost my memories?

He did that thing again where he kicked the horse like we were in some fucking horse race, but at least I was used to it this time. I didn't fall off last time, and that horse seemed to obey him. It wasn't like we had other methods of transportation, and I didn't want to get surrounded and outnumbered by a gang of cannibal rapists. I still thought there was something unnatural about that horse, but it answered to Aeron and Aeron didn't want to kill me, so I guess the horse wouldn't either.

The cabin Aeron found must have been super remote not to have been looted or recovered by someone else before he got there. It was far away from town, but with the horse running impossibly fast, it didn't take long to get there. Weren't horses supposed to get tired? Like, I didn't think I'd ever been around one before, but shouldn't you give them a break if you would run them this hard?

This horse kept a hard gallop right until I started seeing buildings, then Aeron slowed him to a trot. I couldn't even hear the horse breathing hard like all that running did anything to him. *This wasn't a normal horse.*

Aeron let go of my waist, and his sword just kind of appeared again. Where the fuck did he keep that thing, anyway? Did I want to ask?

"What orifice did you pull that from?" I hissed.

"Shut up and stay alert. Scooter's gang is normally a town over on Fridays, but we don't want to risk them changing their schedule. You will call a swarm of Rage Heads if you don't shut the fuck up."

I snapped my mouth shut and eyed my surroundings. This town looked totally dead. It looked like it had been an old-fashioned town before the world ended, and now it looked like a ghost town. Most of the windows were smashed, and there was dirt everywhere. It looked like Washington State was some sort of desert out here in this city.

As we made our way through this city, I had one big question on my mind. If Aeron and his friends had all the answers and killing one man was the answer to stopping all of this, why the fuck did they let it get so bad? This was just fucking bleak. We were the only living souls in this town except possibly a gang who could be out here looking for someone to rape and eat.

Was *everyone* dead except this Scooter and his gang? I couldn't ask right now because I knew we had to stay quiet. Aeron brought the horse up to a little mom and pop store and dismounted. He helped me down and smacked the horse on the ass. The horse took off. Wasn't that our ride home? Why wasn't he tying it to a post like they did in movies?

"Simpson's Grocery is the only shop I haven't hit up yet. I haven't found a local pharmacy, so there's a good chance it's in that store."

"Where'd our ride home go?"

"To safety. He'd be a sitting duck if I tied him down. He's not the kind of beast you chain up. He'll come when I call him. Now, get your bat ready. The Rage Heads haven't spotted us yet, but there's a ninety-nine percent chance there will be some inside the store. The looters who broke the windows made sure the Rage Heads would be in most places anyone tried to get supplies from later."

Okay, I didn't know much about horses, but that couldn't be a normal horse. I just shrugged. I already knew Aeron would not tell me a fucking thing. The best thing to do was to go with the flow until I couldn't anymore. Aeron would eventually trust me with his secrets, or I would get to the point that I needed to strike out on my own because I figured out he was crazier than a shit house rat.

Aeron held his sword up and moved towards the door. He held his fingers to his lips and reminded me again to be totally quiet. Like I didn't know that by now, but he was talking too like apocalypse rules didn't apply to him.

The lock on the door was long broken. Aeron turned the knob and snuck in on silent feet. I held Smurfette at ready and followed. I should have been scared. I'd seen those things at the hospital. I saw what they did to the staff. I was about to go into a cramped space with just me and a guy I was pretty sure was crazy who had a sword. I had to be insane to be out here with no memories and trusting the first person I met.

But there was something about the blue baseball bat that seemed familiar. There was something about it that made me think I could do anything. Even if I didn't remember shit, I could take on a few cannibal corpses with this thing. And if Aeron and that crazy horse proved to be false friends, I could bash their heads in too.

The store was dim when I stepped inside. The only light was sunlight filtering through the broken glass at the front of the store. I didn't hear that awful wailing noise again, but I could hear the shuffling of feet among debris on the floor.

My heart was racing. I needed to kill these things before they could call for backup. Aeron said they hunted in packs, and that noise I heard called the other Rage Heads. We needed to kill every single one of them in this store before we ended up in some swarm in this cramped space. I already knew I didn't like small spaces.

I didn't focus on the shelves or filling my rucksack. I knew that was the entire reason we were out here, but if I was working with Aeron, we needed to work as a team. Let him fill his rucksack, and I could watch his back killing these things. Or, he could watch mine while I snatched shit, but he had more experience with supply runs than I did, so he knew what to grab.

I turned the corner and spotted one. He wasn't moving fast like the one at the hospital. He was just standing in the center of an empty bread aisle rotting in place. Think, Ariel. Aeron said they hunted by sound and smell. I couldn't do much about what I smelled like, but I could be quiet.

Aeron had grabbed a pair of black stompy boots from my old apartment. They fit like an old friend and were surprisingly quiet on this linoleum floor. I just needed to not step on anything left on the floor. I raised Smurfette and locked my gaze on my prey. It was all well and good being told things about the Rage Heads, but I needed to study them and figure out how to kill them myself.

This one was just standing in the center of the aisle, letting out soft moans. How close could I get to it before it realized I was there and attacked? That was something I needed to learn for myself. I needed to study these dead bastards in their natural environment, so they didn't eat me.

I crept up behind it. Closer and closer. Just a little bit more. I needed to avoid everything on the floor. I got precisely five feet behind it before it whirled around lightning fast and snarled at me. This was a ripe one. One of its eyeballs was dangling out its head. Gross. I needed to bash its head in before it called for more.

The nasty thing lunged at me, and I met it. It was way faster than I was. Whatever mutation these things had made them move much faster than regular humans. I gripped Smurfette and swung. That thing's rotten fingers brushed my forearm right as Smurfette made contact with its head. I heard a sickening crack, and the thing fell over in a heap.

One down. How many were in here? I made my way to the end of the aisle. This would be so much easier if I had a way to communicate with Aeron. I saw black blood spreading at the end of the aisle. Aeron must have gotten one with his sword. I stepped around the blood and found a headless corpse. I kicked its head away and kept going.

There was the deader Rage Head. Where was Aeron? Shouldn't we check-in? I looked down the next aisle. There was another headless Rage Head. Well, shit. Aeron killed two, and I only had one. I was slacking. I moved as quietly as I could, making my way to the back of the store while checking for the Rage Heads. I didn't find any that needed to be killed. Aeron had gotten most of them.

I met him at the very back by a pharmacy counter.

"We hit the jackpot. It looks like most people hit the other grocery store here and focused on raiding the pharmacy. I will still hit up the pharmacy and see if there's anything good. Clearing out a pharmacy is hard if there's anything in there because space is always smaller, and the shelves are cramped. You never know when you step inside if it's just one, or the place is filled with them."

I knew why we had to do this, but could I also say I hated the idea of going into a cramped space with these things? I knew Aeron had done this alone countless times and could probably do this without me, but I couldn't exactly tell him I wasn't going in there with him because I had claustrophobia.

I would have to nut up, deal with it, and go in there even if the idea made me want to nope right out of this entire store. I took a deep breath.

"What's the strategy for going in there? I don't know about before, but right now, I have a problem with small spaces. I'm going in there anyway, but it would make things a lot easier if I knew there was a plan."

"There is a plan. I go in, and you stay out. Go out to the rest of the store and start filling your rucksack. Monitor the rest of the store for Rage Heads sneaking through the windows or Scooter's gang making a surprise visit to the town."

"Shouldn't I help now that I'm here?"

"You are helping by getting supplies and keeping watch. Let me deal with the pharmacy. We'll tag team it."

I knew he was just making me feel better. What happened to me that I had such a problem with small spaces? Did Aeron know, and he wasn't telling me? At least I was helping a little.

I set back into the store and started exploring. There were some canned goods still left, but they were dented, and the label was long gone. It wouldn't hurt to grab them, anyway. For all I knew, I was grabbing nothing but canned tomatoes, but if Aeron could hunt deer, we could find a way to make deer stew with it. We couldn't exactly be picky. Maybe some of these were canned pears. I just had this feeling I used to like pears.

I went towards the back of the store. There was a lone jumbo box of tampons. Aeron might not need that shit, but I did, and if he said anything about them being a necessity, I would shove one up his nose while he slept. No one called off periods during the apocalypse, though someone probably should. It was only fair.

The store was pretty bleak. I hoped Aeron had better luck than I did. I got a bunch of unlabeled cans and my tampons. My rucksack was full, but Aeron hadn't come out of the pharmacy yet. I decided to check on him. He said tag team it. I was tagging him by checking on his ass, even if he probably didn't need me.

The pharmacy door was open, and I didn't hear any sounds from inside.

"Aeron?" I hissed.

Nothing.

"You grumpy asshole, are you alive in there?"

He'd better not be dead. If he were just playing games with me, then I'd make him dead. I stepped inside the pharmacy, and it felt like someone had sucked the oxygen from the room. My heart was pounding in my ears, and I felt like I would vomit. All my instincts were screaming at me to get the fuck out of here, but if Aeron was in trouble, I needed to find him.

I took a step forward, and it was like black spots started clouding my vision. I was getting dizzy. The walls were closing in on me, and this room was getting even smaller. I needed to get the fuck out of there, but I also needed to find Aeron. My foot felt like lead as I tried to move it forward. My feet wanted to be running out of there, and I was forcing them onward.

There was this pounding in my ears, and the black spots were increasing. I tried to ignore it. What if Aeron was hurt? I needed to know if he was dead. I needed to see it. If he was a Rage Head now, then I needed to give him peace. I just needed to find him.

I saw him through the haze of black spots in my vision. He was alive, and he had this look of panic in his eyes. That was for me, I thought. He went running towards me like he was worried about me instead of me coming in here to check on him.

Aeron caught me right as I passed out.

EIGHT

Something stank, and it differed from the usual rotting apocalypse stank that was in the air now. I heard someone call my name, and then someone *slapped me in the face.* I bolted to a sitting position trying to figure out who I needed to punch. I was lying on the sidewalk outside of the grocery store we just looted in Aeron's lap. And he fucking slapped me.

"What the fuck, Aeron?"

"You tried to come to the pharmacy. You had a panic attack and passed out."

"I did not!"

I already knew I did, but I was embarrassed as fuck it happened. Maybe if I denied it happened, he would pretend like it didn't. I didn't want to be the weakest link in this whole assassination plot. I wasn't sure if I wanted to take part, but I didn't want to get dumped before I figured that out because I couldn't deal with small spaces.

"Ariel, you have serious claustrophobia. You could have helped out better looting the store, and you wouldn't have had to go through that. Why did you come back there, and why didn't you leave when you started having a panic attack?"

"I filled my rucksack, and I thought you'd been gone too long. I was checking on you. I got worried when I called your name, and you didn't answer. I thought you were hurt. What the fuck were you doing, and why didn't you answer?"

"Because I hit the fucking jackpot in that pharmacy. Everyone was so concerned about the meds, and they didn't pay any attention to the locked door in the back. It's an extra storeroom for the grocery store. There are labeled cans, chips, and cookies in there. Dump out your bag. I even found your favorite. They have Cheetos in there!"

Aeron was so excited about his find, but I couldn't remember a thing about liking Cheetos. Maybe when I ate them, I would have another flash of my past life. This was good. Aeron found a stash we could use, I learned a little about killing Rage Heads, and I discovered I couldn't handle small spaces at all without fainting. I'd have to get over the whole small spaces shit fast because I was sure I would have to hide in some, eventually.

Aeron helped me to my feet this time and led me back into the store.

"See if you can find more bags. I'll load everything in the supply closet up. Stand watch and don't come back in the pharmacy."

I felt seriously unhelpful as I just stood there and watched the door and a broken window. He spent all the time casing this place and learning the local gang's raiding schedule. He was the one that found the secret stash. I got a bunch of dented cans. I was pretty lousy at this whole apocalypse thing, but at least I managed to kill one of them. And I found some bags so Aeron could bring more home with us.

Aeron finally came out with both of our rucksacks and two garbage bags full of stuff. He also had this massive smile on his face like he just stopped the apocalypse. He handed me the backpack and one of the garbage bags, and we stepped outside. The horse was standing there waiting for us like he knew we just finished. I knew he wasn't standing outside when I was watching the window. That wasn't a normal fucking horse. The horse knew that I knew that too because I swear it just winked at me again.

Aeron tied our haul to the saddle and helped me up a little more gracefully this time. I felt less like a sack of potatoes this time. He climbed up behind me, and I didn't even react when the horse took off running like a bat out of Hell. I just expected it. The horse was some sort of devil horse, and it answered to Aeron. And I agreed to trust Aeron. Somehow, I got the feeling that wasn't the dumbest thing I'd ever done in my life. I mean, I had a baby blue baseball bat I named Smurfette. There was a good chance I had been pretty fucking weird before I lost my memories.

The ride back to the cabin was long, and Aeron pushed the horse pretty hard. And I got this weird feeling the horse liked it too. I got this vibe off the horse it enjoyed riding hard and fast into some sort of battle where it got to trample people with those enormous hooves of his.

I got this flash in my head, and I had no idea where it came from. It couldn't be a memory because it wasn't possible. I saw Aeron sitting on top of that horse, but he was different. His hair was longer and flowing in waves down his back. The sword he always carried was in flames, but it wasn't burning him on the horse. The horse's eyes were glowing red like I'd seen flashes of.

This is where the impossible came in. Aeron's eyes were glowing white, and there was this white glow that was coming from his body. He also had this huge set of white wings coming from his back like an angel.

I shook my head, and the image went away. Now was not the time to be having sexual fantasies about the crazy conspiracy theory nut who saved my life. He hadn't shown me a single shred of proof he wasn't some nutter who thought he was the world's savior.

Even though Aeron helped me on the horse nicely, he practically threw me on the ground, helping me off. He untied our bag and gave the devil horse another smack on the ass. When he turned to look at me, he seemed as happy as a kindergartner who just got told they could finger paint for the entire day.

"I found chips, Velveeta, and a jar of salsa. We're having fucking *nachos* for dinner, Speedy."

I may not remember eating nachos, but I knew only heathens didn't like nachos. I squealed and jumped up and down. I had this weird urge to hug him, but I had this feeling he wouldn't like it, and I didn't want to ruin the moment.

I held my hand up for a fist bump instead.

"Thank god you looked in that closet then! Nachos during the apocalypse!"

"Nachos for dinner. Tomorrow, we rough it and head out to meet Leif in Mexico."

"He's the one who specializes in diseases?"

"Yes. I know you think I'm insane, but he can show you his research and prove to you we are on the right path.

Hopefully, you will have gotten back more of your memories by then."

"Why am I so claustrophobic?"

"Let's not talk about unpleasantness tonight, Ariel. Come on, nachos!"

I didn't learn why I had such a problem with small spaces, but I did learn one thing about myself right then and there. I could be bribed with melty, fake orange cheese.

Nine

Nachos are a million times sweeter when you know there's no chance in Hell you will ever eat them again, and they trigger a memory. My softball team was called The Amazing Flying Bitches, and we ate them after every game. That was our thing. After the game, we'd hit up the concession stand for nachos and beer. What were the chances of finding beer at the end of the world? I mean, we found plastic cheese and made nachos. It could happen, right?

Aeron was pleasant over dinner. He was so happy about our haul, and he forgot to be a dick. He even cracked a few jokes. If he kept this up, I might even start to like him a little. We kept the conversation away from his past. I didn't press because I knew it was a touchy subject.

We were cramming nachos in our faces, and I was way past the point of being full, but I would not stop eating because I might never get this again.

"What do you think happened to my softball team? When I got that flash after the softball game, we all seemed close. When I was looking through my clothes, I got a flash at a concert with a girl from my team everyone called Pokey."

"We can check. I was planning on bringing you to your old apartment on the way to Mexico. There might be things you want to take, and it'll probably jog some memories loose. Isaiah is the President of the United States, but not everyone follows him. A lot of the gangs have established themselves as either governors or kings. Some governors cooperate with him, and the kings do whatever the fuck they want. Scooter fancies himself the King of Washington, but there's already a governor in one of the larger cities, and he answers to Isaiah. There's just not enough military to crush people like Scooter."

"Do you have any proof Isaiah is responsible for all of this other than the fact that he was the majority share-holder in that company? What does he get out of turning the world into this? He's president of one country, and he doesn't even have a military behind him. It sounds like a lot of the country doesn't even recognize him as president. What's the point?"

"Does anyone need a reason to cause the end of the world?"

"Well, yeah. There's no way to do it without dying along with everyone else. Even if he locks himself in the White House, he will die a horrible death with everyone else."

Aeron just shrugged.

"Why do serial killers kill people and dictators commit mass genocide? They eventually get caught and pay for their crimes. People do what they are programmed to do. Isaiah was programmed to do this."

I scoffed.

"I don't believe that. He probably has mommy issues."

Aeron started laughing.

"Close. Daddy issues. As I said, there are things deeply ingrained in all of us. I was programmed to end this, just like Leif is programmed to be good with diseases, Asher is good at justice and conquest, and Dice is good at war strategy. We were put together for a reason."

"What am I programmed for?" I asked.

"You're a wild card, Ariel. You could help us end this."

"How? I'm just a girl from Los Angeles."

"You're so much more than that, Ariel, and I wish I could tell you why without totally breaking your mind. I was hoping you'd have your memories if I ever found you. You should get to bed. We have to start out early in the morning to avoid any gangs on our way out of Washington."

Fuck. I thought I was getting somewhere I might find out something. I had no idea what Aeron meant about people being programmed and me being a wildcard. What did that even mean? I was so frustrated because I knew I would not find out for a long time. My memories would have to come back for Aeron to tell me certain things, and they were only coming in bits and pieces.

I knew this conversation was over, so I left and went to my bedroom. I changed back into my yoga pants and slipped under the covers. I rested Smurfette on the pillow next to me. I already knew there was no way I could sleep unless she were next to me.

I got a memory back when I was sleeping before. Maybe I'd get one again. Hopefully, it wouldn't be a nightmare this time.

TEN

I am four years old. I've been dropped off at the bad place again. A man I love just walked away while I plead for him to stay. I can't see his face. Only the back of his suit. The two nasty men in lab coats drag me back to a room. It's the one room I don't want to go to. There is pain in this room. This is the bad room.

I can see the machine in the center of the room. It's small. It's my size. It's just big enough for a four-year-old, and it's filled with needles. When I see it, I fight. I fight every time they want to put me in the bad machine. It never works. They are so much bigger than I am.

I will beat them this time. I'm not going in the machine. I manage to break free and run for the door. There's a keypad to get out. I'm too short to reach it. My small fists pound on the door as I scream for someone to help me.

The bad machine is loud. There are bright lights and a dome of needles. When they turn it on, there is a pounding noise and a bright light that hurts my eyes. The worst part is *the needles. The needles press down and puncture my young flesh, even in my face. That is not happening to me today.*

Someone grabs me from behind, and I scream. They press their hands over my mouth and nose, and I can hardly breathe. They want me awake on the days they put me in the machine. Sometimes, when I fight, they will inject me with things that make me sleepy, but never on the days they use the bad machine.

I can't fight it. Two men hold me down as they strap me into the machine. They bring the cover down. I hear the pounding as it's turned on. The bright lights start flashing. The needles come down towards my face.

I woke up screaming. Why couldn't my memories ever be pleasant? Aeron kicked the door down and stood in the door frame without a shirt on. I thought he would yell at me for being too noisy, but I saw a look of concern on his face.

"Was it an awful memory?"

I was still shaking, and there were tears on my face.

"If that was real, I know why I have a problem with small spaces now."

Aeron's breath hitched.

"I'm sorry, Ariel. Do you want me to stay?"

Did I? I wasn't sure how much sleep I had gotten or what time it was. I knew I wasn't getting back to sleep after that nightmare. I could really use the company.

"Yeah, can you?"

Aeron moved Smurfette so she was right between us and laid on top of the covers right next to me. This was so fucking awkward.

"Was that real?" I asked.

"Yes, it was."

"What was the point of that terrible machine?"

"To take your blood while you were scared."

"Why would someone do that to me?"

"It was part of a clinical trial. Your father signed you up. It was all very hush-hush, and they were eventually shut down."

"What were they trying to achieve torturing children? And why can't I see my father's face in all these memories?"

"I suppose I can tell you this. You ended up hating your father. You got emancipated when you were fifteen and lived away from him. You put yourself through college and were a hard worker."

I was glad I ended up hating that fucker because when I was getting memories in my dreams, all I could feel was that I loved him, even if he was just walking away and leaving me in that terrible place. I hoped I eventually paid that bastard back for what he did to me when I was a child.

"Will you tell me what I majored in?"

Aeron always avoided touching me. When he had to, he did things like heaving me on his horse. His finger traced one of the cards on my arm. The Alice in Wonderland sleeves weren't based on the Disney cartoons or the drawings from the book. They were totally original drawings. It was like a deck of cards exploded from my wrist, and characters from the Alice books intertwined with cards and roses.

"You majored in art. You drew these, you know. I'm surprised you haven't gotten the urge to draw."

I held my arm up and studied the art on my arm. Had I drawn this? That was pretty fucking cool. What else could I do?

"Is there a way to get a pen and paper? If I can draw,

maybe if I just sat there with a blank piece of paper and a pen, something might come out."

Aeron was lying next to me like a stick of wood. He wasn't even looking at me. His arms were crossed over his chest, and he was staring straight up at the ceiling.

"It's a good idea. The only place I can think of that might have the blank paper is your old apartment, if squatters haven't moved in."

"I lived in Los Angeles, didn't I?"

"Yes, you did."

"Aeron? Was I at that research facility when you found me because my father was experimenting on me again?"

Aeron looked like he wanted to say something, then stopped. Someone experimented on me when I was a child, and I somehow ended up at one again as an adult. Whatever happened there, I lost my memories. Did something happen there that was so horrible, I didn't just block that out, I blocked everything out?

"They weren't experimenting on you there, Ariel. Please, don't ask me more questions. We have to be up early in the morning, and we have a long day of travel ahead of us. Do you think you can get back to sleep?"

"Aeron, I have a million questions—"

"I know. And you'll get them in time. Please, what can I do to get you to sleep?"

"I don't know."

I didn't. Nothing would help me sleep right now. I was too keyed up. What the fuck happened to me, anyway?

Aeron started singing softly. He had a good voice— soft and smooth with just the right amount of vibrato. As much as I didn't want to, I felt my eyes getting heavier and heavier. Eventually, I fell asleep.

Eleven

As gentle as Aeron was singing me some sort of lullaby when I had a bad dream, he was now trying to wake me up by poking the shit out of me and yelling in my face. Why couldn't he be as sweet as last night all the time? He said people were programmed to act a certain way. Where was his switch to turn off asshole mode?

I kept my eyes closed like I was still sleeping. I let out this groan like I would not wake up, even though his finger jabbing into my ribs had long woken me up. My hand darted out to the pillow. I didn't think this would work, but I pounced and tried to smack him in the face with the pillow.

Ha! I got him right in the nose. Aeron jumped out of bed and scowled at me.

"Be serious. We're about to head out on the open road. I need you alert, so you don't get us both killed."

"Then don't poke me like that. It hurts, and I don't like it. Is there something wrong with waking me up like a normal person?"

Aeron started grumbling, and I couldn't make out some things he was muttering.

"Get dressed and come out to the kitchen to eat. We need to leave soon."

I sighed and rubbed the sleep out of my eyes. Someone had blacked out all the windows in this cabin, so I couldn't even imagine if it was still dark out. Was there something wrong with me? I'd seen my reflection the first time I showered. I wasn't totally gross looking. If you were into tattooed girls with pink hair, I could be considered arm candy in certain circles. Aeron treated me like I was repulsive. I knew he was poking me like that because it was the best way to wake me with as little contact as possible. Was he worried he would catch girl cooties?

Aeron could suck my left nut. If his friends were as bad as he was, they could kill the president on their own. I got dressed and stomped into the kitchen. I wasn't expecting a miracle for breakfast, but I smelled it as soon as I stepped in.

"No, shit. Pancakes?"

"Yeah. I found a jar of maple syrup in the supply closet. It goes without saying we won't have nachos again, but as long as supplies last, I can make pancakes over a campfire. You may get sick of them."

I dug into the syrupy maple goodness and shoved it in my face. I moaned at the taste.

"I have this feeling I'm not going to get sick of these."

Aeron cocked an eyebrow at me and looked totally uncomfortable.

"Do you always make sex noises when you eat? You did it with the nachos too."

"What? Who knows when the last time I've eaten

was? You won't tell me how long I was at that facility, and I can't remember."

"Don't get used to this, Ariel. I'm good at finding food, but there will be times we are eating out of mystery cans, and that's it. Sometimes, I find nothing when I'm hunting, and it's rare I find a cabin like this. Sometimes, I do find a cabin with a generator, but then I can't find gas."

"Yeah, I get it. I'm enjoying it while I have it. You should loosen up and make sex noises when you eat too. Come on, nachos and pancakes during the apocalypse? That can be better than sex."

Okay, Aeron was a total prude. He didn't like the happy noises I made when I ate, and as soon as I mentioned sex, he totally closed up and left the room.

"I will make sure we pack everything."

I had nachos. I suppose it was too much to ask that the hot guy who found me was also a little kinky. I'd settle for him being a little sweeter. For now, I was just going to enjoy these delicious pancakes and stop wishing for what I didn't have. Aeron was who he was, grumpy fuck and all.

Aeron didn't come back in until I was long done with my breakfast, and he had already saddled the horse and tied all our bags to the saddle.

"What's the deal with your horse?"

"We don't have time for this, Ariel. Just know when it comes down to it, Meremoth will save your life. Now, shut up so we can leave."

I guess we were back to that. Aeron put me on the back of his horse like I was some infected Rage Head that he didn't want to touch. A girl could get a complex at some point. Aeron hopped up behind me and kicked the horse again. We took off at that incredibly fast pace.

"Don't you need to pace your horse?"

"The only way out of town to California is straight through Scooter's territory. Meremoth can handle it. I told you, Scooter's gang is heavily armed, and there are scouts everywhere. Now, be quiet, so we don't get shot at."

Let's all have a moment of silence and pray that this crazy demonic horse could get us the Hell out of this town before rapist cannibals started taking potshots at us. Smurfette was good at smashing brains, but she wasn't a long-range weapon, and neither was Aeron's sword. Who still fought with swords, anyway?

Meremoth galloped through a dead town at a punishing pace. I gripped the pommel, and Aeron held my waist, so I didn't fall off. We cut back through the main area that we looted and got on a road I didn't recognize.

I realized we were about to go deep into the shit when Aeron's grip on my waist tightened. My eyes darted left and right, taking in my surroundings. I knew there was a good chance I wouldn't be able to see them, but they could see me, and I didn't like that.

I was gripping Smurfette with my free hand and holding her across the saddle. She would be useless against a gun in the distance, but it was still comforting to have her with me. Where was everyone? I didn't even see Rage Heads out here. They were fast, but they weren't as fast as Meremoth. Still, I didn't want a whole herd of them chasing us.

I finally saw three Rage Heads milling about in the distance, and I'll be totally fucked, but Aeron slowed the damned horse down and started yelling.

"What are you doing?" I hissed.

He had their attention now. They trained their red eyes on us, and I could hear their moans in the distance.

"Come and get it, assholes!" Aeron yelled.

This fucker would get me eaten. The three Rage Heads let out that wail like they were signaling for backup, and Aeron was just sitting on the back of his demonic horse and not getting us out of there. More Rage Heads started spilling out of the trees to see what the big fuss was. The road became this entire choir of Rage Head wails, and this was definitely a concert I didn't want to attend.

"Free meal!" Aeron yelled, kicking Meremoth again.

This mother fucker right here. Did he take me out of that clinic and feed me nachos as a last meal so I could get eaten to death with him? And pancakes? Was that a trick too? Clearly, trusting anyone during the end of the world was a bad idea. He probably didn't even know how all this started.

Meremoth took off running, and we had an entire herd of Rage Heads wailing behind us. It terrified me. My blood was pumping, and I was imagining how awful it was to be pulled from a horse and getting eaten alive. I kept trying to look behind us to see how close those things were getting.

Aeron gripped my stomach and nudged me with his shoulder.

"Eyes up ahead, and this will make sense."

Nothing made sense ever since I woke up in that clinic. Like inciting a bunch of mutated corpses to chase us would ever make sense.

"Look up ahead. It's right there, Ariel," Aeron growled, digging his nails in my waist.

That was when I saw it—some sort of makeshift

settlement. There were watchtowers, and there were men with guns manning the two towers. The settlement looked like it spread out for most of the woods too. We had two options. Take a longer way around and run into a massive herd of Rage Heads, or go straight through Scooter's settlement.

And this crazy mother fucker behind me decided to go straight through with a herd of Rage Heads chasing us. I could hear them screeching behind us. It kept building the further we ran, and the more they screeched, the bigger the herd got. What would stop them from chasing us all the way to California? Aeron had better have thought this through further than getting past the guns.

And that roadblock in front of the settlement. We were barreling towards a barricade made of wooden spikes at an alarming speed. Someone at the camp was ringing a bell, and men with guns were spilling out of the houses. There were at least a hundred shotguns pointed right at us, and I'm sure we made some sort of fucked up sight. A girl on a horse with a blue baseball bat and a crazy man with a sword being followed by an army of dead cannibals. I kind of wished I was back in a coma.

Aeron pulled me to his chest.

"Hold on tight, Speedy!" he yelled as we raced towards that death trap in the middle of the road.

I held onto the pommel for dear life and shrieked bloody murder, and Meremoth went sailing over that bloody road trap like he was some sort of Pegasus. I could hear the squelch of bodies being impaled on the wooden spikes, and then I heard wood splintering as it broke.

Gunshots rang out. Most of them were aimed at the Rage Heads, but a few people shot at us at first. I felt a bullet just barely miss my ear before the sounds of men screaming started filling my ears. Scooter's gang became more concerned with saving their own lives than killing us.

The sounds of gunshots, screams, and wails of the dead were getting further in the distance, but Meremoth was still running like we were being chased. That damned horse never seemed to get tired, and I didn't think a regular horse could have cleared that roadblock with two people on its back.

Meremoth didn't slow down until we saw a sign that we had entered a new city. Aeron reached around me and patted his neck.

"Good boy."

"Are we allowed to talk now?" I snapped. "Because you are fucking insane. You could have got us killed."

"I'll never get us killed, Speedy. I'm your best shot at living through this. I told you my specialty was death. Scooter's gang are nasty people. They've either raped or eaten everyone in that city or the surrounding cities. I did the world a favor and saved your life. They would have done worse to you if they had caught you."

Who the fuck was I spending my apocalypse with?

Twelve

We ran like the devil getting out of that city, but we took a lazy walk for the rest of the day. Most of the herd of Rage Heads stayed behind to eat Scooter's gang. We walked in total silence. Aeron never was much of a talker, and I was mad at him about that stunt for most of the ride.

But the more we walked, the more I found my anger dissipating. It worked, and was what was left of humanity really better off with Scooter and his gang in the world? Not really. If they had come at me, I would have killed as many of them as I could, but I saw how many people were living there. There were way more of them than there were of us. Something was still bothering me.

"Was there no other way to get out of that town besides right through the front door of Scooter's territory?"

"Not without adding two days to our journey, and if we did that, there would be no safe place for us to sleep. We could do it my way and take some evil people out of the equation so some living stood a better chance or we could have tried to go the long way and risked one of Scooter's men finding us or being discovered by a herd of Rage Heads."

"You still should have told me that's what you were planning."

Aeron let out a chuckle.

"You would never have gotten on Meremoth, and we'd still be back at the cabin fighting."

"I don't like surprises."

"I know."

"So, what's next?"

"I have safe houses the entire way to Mexico. Provided they haven't been discovered, we should be safe there. We'll have to make sure no Rage Heads have broken the perimeter and gotten in. Some of them are one-bedroom, so we must share a bed unless you want to sleep on the couch."

This guy right here. Didn't most guys offer to take the couch when there was only one bed? What a gentleman. Well, I wasn't sleeping on the couch either. It was the fucking apocalypse. There were walking corpses everywhere, and there would be times I was eating out of a can. I was sure I'd end up sleeping on dirt floors or the woods. If there was a bed, I was taking what I could get. Besides, Aeron seemed way more uncomfortable being around me than I was with him, and I owed him a little payback for that stunt with Scooter's gang. Apparently, I was a passive-aggressive little bitch before I lost my memories.

"I'm sleeping in the fucking bed, Aeron."

I felt him sigh against my back.

"I had a feeling you would say that."

"*You* can take the couch if you don't want to sleep next to me."

"That couch is all lumpy and has seen better days."

"And you wanted me to sleep on it? Dick."

We rode all day, and we only stopped so Meremoth could drink water and eat. My ass was killing me. We only got off the back of the demon horse so he could have a break. We stopped at a creek while Meremoth drank and grazed. Aeron and I got to eat our haul from the storeroom.

Aeron triumphantly whipped something from his bag and shoved it right in my face.

"I was saving this, but you're being cranky. I found Cheetos!"

He was about to smash the bag of Cheetos right into my nose. I snatched the bag away from him and tore it open. I was starving.

"I have every right to be cranky, asshole. You got us chased by a bunch a cannibal corpses so you could kill some cannibal humans."

Aeron whipped out a bag of Funyuns and gave me this shit-eating grin.

"Yeah, but it fucking worked. Eat your Cheetos, Ariel."

"You aren't always going to be able to bribe me with orange cheese, you know."

Aeron leaned back against the tree with his Funyuns. He closed his eyes like Funyuns were his Kryptonite. He had this dreamy look on his face like he did when we were pigging out on nachos. Note to self—look for Funyuns when we were out looting.

He said I liked Cheetos, and he saved these just for me. In a way, it was probably the nicest thing he'd ever done for me, aside from singing me to sleep. I popped one in my mouth and chewed. Oh, my god. When the popped corn and powdered orange cheese hit my tongue, I nearly came. I closed my eyes and just savored it.

"You're doing it again," Aeron said, snapping me out of my cheese reverie.

"What?" I asked, sucking all the powdered cheese off my fingers.

"You're making sex noises."

"Well, I apparently like food, and it's not like I'm getting laid any time soon. You hate me. I'm not sure why you're so insistent I come with you to kill the president. It's not like there are any other options out there right now."

"Who said I hate you?"

"You treat everyone like dirt, cupcake."

Aeron's mouth hung open with a Funyun poised to go right in.

"I don't treat you like dirt. I got you nachos and Cheetos."

"Yeah, you did, but you're still gruff with me sometimes."

"Nachos don't impress you? Getting those during the apocalypse is almost impossible."

Was Aeron... trying to impress me with his storeroom haul? This whole time, I thought the nachos and pancakes were because he wanted them and needed to eat too, but was that Aeron's way of being kind to me?

"The nachos, pancakes, and Cheetos are pretty fucking impressive, cowboy."

"Then, what more do you want, Ariel?"

"You never talk to me, and when you do, you act like you don't want to."

Aeron ran his fingers through his pale blond hair.

"It's not that I don't want to, Ariel. Your memory loss

is tricky. If I say the wrong thing, all of your memories will flood back in at once, and the damage would be irreversible. I say little because I have less of a chance of hurting you."

"You can't even make bullshit talk about the weather?"

Aeron laughed and resumed mowing his way through his Funyuns.

"Fair enough. We can chat about that."

"Apparently, orange cheese is my weakness. Are those Funyuns yours?"

"Close. Have you ever had one of those fried onion blossoms with just the right dipping sauce? I'd walk through a herd of Rage Heads just to get one right about now."

I laughed. Now, we were getting somewhere.

"I'm pretty sure I have, even if I can't remember when. Maybe we can make onion blossoms happen. Who knows? I mean, we had nachos."

"Nachos are right up there as a top favorite food too, so let's just settle for that. Where we are going tonight doesn't have a generator, so it'll be the junk food I took from the closet and cans. It's not safe to meet with Cougar for trade that late."

"Cougar?"

"She's kind of the mayor. The town we are stopping in isn't like the one we left. They've secured their borders to keep the Rage Heads and people like Scooter out. I had to work my ass off to be allowed inside. When we get to the gate, don't speak unless spoken to. I must vouch for you before they allow you inside."

"What city are we stopping in?"

"Before or after the war? Cities and states don't really

exist anymore. I gave you the city you would have known before, but it's not called that anymore. The settlement we are going to is called Gabriel's Haven. Cougar runs the place."

"Does everyone go by nicknames now? Cougar, Scooter. Is your name even Aeron?"

"You're worried about nicknames, Speedy?"

Did Aeron just make a joke? He was smirking like he did. I laughed.

"Fair enough, but everyone has a nickname in roller derby. Don't ask me how I know that."

"Many people decided that the world was ending, the government had fallen, and nothing was the same. Their lives would never be the same and some of them were stepping up and adopting identities they never would have before. Why not take a new name? Cougar taught kindergarten before all of this."

I waved a Cheeto at him and started my rant. I didn't even know where the fuck it was coming from.

"Of course, the well-run, secure city is head up by a woman and a teacher. I hope those assholes she's keeping safe appreciate her more than people did before the apocalypse."

Aeron dusted Funyun dust off his fingers.

"Oh, trust me. She's respected and feared by every single person in Gabriel's Haven. She's a real hardass. She's got a barter system set up, and they've even got crops growing. We need to get going if we will make it there before it gets dark."

I sighed. Baby steps. I would eventually get to the bottom of Aeron with no last name.

THIRTEEN

The ride to Gabriel's Haven was long, but at least Aeron talked to me this time as long as we kept the conversation totally neutral. He wouldn't talk about me, and even though talking about himself would not trigger my memories, he wouldn't talk about himself. Instead, he told me all about the settlement at Gabriel's Haven. It sounded like they had a marvelous thing going, but it wasn't the norm around the world. The world had divided itself between the Cougars and the Scooters of the world, and the Scooters were always trying to take over settlements like Gabriel's Haven.

I thought the death trap in front of Scooter's territory was big, but it was nowhere near what they had at Gabriel's Haven. It looked like they had raided every possible building and pulled down steel panels for their ten-foot-high fence, which was also lined with barbed wire. It spread out as far as I could see.

Aeron pulled Meremoth up to the gate and just stopped. Two large rifles popped over a break in the fence.

"State your business!"

"It's Aeron, and I have a guest."

He had to announce himself? How did they not recognize that fucking horse if they couldn't see his face? I heard another voice over the fence.

"Aeron? He's cool, Jake. Let him through, and we'll vet his guest."

"That you, Edward?" Aeron yelled. "Since when are you not at the fence?"

"Jake is in training. I have to sleep sometime, and we need all the eyes we can get. We found the item you wanted on a scouting trip. You got anything good to trade for it?"

"Yeah, I do."

The gate swung open, and Meremoth took us inside. I got my first look at Gabriel's Haven. As far as apocalypse cities went, it looked pretty well run. The houses were neat, and I didn't see a broken window in sight. They had managed to get some vegetables growing in soil that had seen better days, and it looked like they had a water filtration system set up. In the event of an apocalypse, teachers really should run everything.

But I wasn't welcome here just yet. I was a stranger, and these people didn't know if I would ruin the tranquil life they had carved out here. I had about twenty guns aimed at my head as soon as the gate closed.

A regal-looking woman in her sixties came up and sized me up. I felt like a child who had done something wrong, and she could just reach into my mind and pluck my sin right out of me.

"Who is the stray, Aeron?"

"A precious package who can help me right some wrongs."

What the fuck?

"Yes, your theory about the water has proven true. We've stayed away from certain brands of bottled water on our raids. None of the children have mutated since we took your advice. I know your plan is this big secret. This slip of a thing can help you with that?"

Were people still having children during the apocalypse? Why not? I suppose condoms were scarce, and there wasn't much else to do. It wasn't like you could Netflix and chill anymore. All you could do was the chill part. I suppose I'd be getting my chill on too if I had a pack of condoms and more options than a guy who seemed repulsed when he touched me. I'd take my orange cheese for now. Sex was way too much to ask for.

"Yes, she can. We'll only be here for the night. We need to meet part of my team in Mexico."

Everyone started moaning and groaning. Cougar just cocked an eyebrow at him.

"Only the night? You usually stay longer."

"I'll be back, Cougar. And this time with more than just things to barter."

"What's the girl's name?"

"Speedy."

"I've been saving that item you wanted for when you returned. We actually hit the jackpot in this house we hit, and there was plenty to go around."

Aeron was grinning like he just heard the best news of his life.

"Good, because I hit the jackpot back in Scooter's territory and can make the trade worth your while."

"And Scooter let you leave with it? With a pretty girl with you?"

"Scooter won't be bothering you anymore."

"With you, I don't want to know, but we are grateful,

like always. Go get the girl settled, and I'll send Steven to negotiate the barter."

Aeron groaned.

"Do you always have to send the one former lawyer when we barter?"

Cougar just grinned.

"Have to make sure the trade is fair. Now, get that sexy ass of yours out of my sight. It's almost curfew."

Aeron did that thing where he smacked Meremoth on the ass, and the horse did that disappearing thing. There might be a curfew for humans in Gabriel's Haven, but they apparently had no problems with a demonic horse on the loose.

Aeron grabbed my hand and started tugging me towards the back of town. His house was way towards the back, and I didn't need to ask why he had this house. Families were living here, and when Aeron was here, he was usually by himself. They didn't have to give him a house since he didn't live here full time. But they did, and it was a one-bedroom with basic necessities if you didn't count the lack of electricity.

Aeron flung the door open and started lighting some gas camping lamps that were scattered around the place.

"What's this big mysterious thing you had them searching for?"

"Wait and see."

"You know I don't like surprises."

"You'll like this one."

I got the feeling in the past I didn't like any surprises, good or bad. There was a knock on the door, and Aeron went running like this surprise had to be better than nachos or Cheetos. Aeron let a small, wiry man in who had something in a box. Of course, it had to be gift wrapped.

They sat at the small dining room table like they were at the Yalta Conference instead of just trading what we all looted. I sat next to them because what the fuck did I know about bartering stolen goods during the apocalypse? I didn't want to ruin this. I was just going to watch and keep my mouth shut.

Steven slid the box across the table.

"It's unopened. We lost some men getting this."

Aeron steepled his fingers, and his gray eyes glittered like he was enjoying every minute of this.

"From what Cougar said, you found enough to go around. And I took out Scooter."

"Don't be nasty, Aeron. Fair is fair. You know Cougar won't like it if you shaft her on a trade."

"Oh, I have no intention of shafting her. But I know she sends you in when she wants to get greedy, and I have no intention of being the one getting shafted."

Steven fell out laughing.

"Welcome back, Aeron. Still, you know she will want something good for this."

"How does Doritos and chocolate sound?"

Wait, Aeron had chocolate and was holding out on me? Whatever was in that box had better be worth it. Were we giving up all the chocolate? I had questions.

"How the fuck did you manage to find that?"

"How did you manage to find enough of what's in that box for the entire community?"

"Found a Rage Head barricaded in his basement with a whole supply and massive amounts of MREs. If he had stuck to the liquor instead of the bottled water he had stockpiled, he might not have turned. He had some brands you warned us about."

"Doomsdayer? Did you get a lot of ammo?"

"Oh, yeah. We got guns, ammo, MREs, canned goods, and some nudie mags for the men. It took several trips, but that Rage Head was fairly fresh, and it was a cramped space. He got his teeth in three of us before we could kill him, and there's no cure for a bite."

"Supply runs can turn shitty in an instant. Do you want to stay and pour one out for them?"

Steven just gave him this crooked grin.

"No. I got my own. I got some MREs and girly mags out of the haul. Cougar has been fiending for some chocolate. She's had us looking on our runs. The most we've found is that nasty baker's chocolate you can't eat. Samantha tried to make brownies with it on the fire since we have flour, but sugar is one thing we don't have."

"Well, tell Cougar she's got her chocolate. I swiped an entire box of Snickers."

And he was just trading them? There had better be something *delicious* in that box. If there was a shitty surprise in that box, I would be upset. I was already questioning Aeron's sanity with this whole killing the president, but if he was just handing out Snickers for mystery boxes, then he was definitely totally insane.

Steven held out his hand.

"You've got yourself a trade."

Aeron went to one of the saddlebags and took out the chocolate and Doritos he was hiding from me. If I knew there was chocolate hidden in there, I probably already would have torn into it and ruined this trade. There'd better be something *outstanding* in that box.

Steven gathered all that beautiful chocolate and disappeared. I was left with Aeron and his mystery box. He was stroking the damned thing like it was his favorite pet.

"What's so special that you gave away chocolate during the end of the world?"

Aeron ripped off the top of the box and triumphantly held up a bottle of Wild Turkey. I cocked an eyebrow at him.

"All that for booze?"

"We're in a safe place to get drunk. Think of it as a way to forget the apocalypse and feel good for a night."

"I've forgotten everything, remember?" I reminded him.

Aeron waved the bottle at me.

"Then let's forget forgetting."

I just shrugged.

"I'll drink to that."

Aeron got two glasses down, but we didn't have many options for mixing. We were basically doing straight shots. Aeron was a big guy. He was bigger than I was in every way. I didn't know much about my past, but I apparently had the tolerance of a linebacker. Aeron was getting pretty sloppy, and I was barely buzzed. We had drunk half the bottle, and I was putting a lid on this. We didn't need to drink the entire thing just because we had it, and I had no desire to hold Aeron's hair back while he puked in the dark.

I helped Aeron to bed and tried to tuck him in. He straight up grabbed me and pulled me into bed. He yanked me to his chest and threw his leg over me. I could feel him nuzzling my neck with his nose.

"You're so pretty," he sighed.

"You're so drunk, Aeron."

"Shut up. Tonight, we forget everything. I'm forgetting you remember nothing. I just want to hold you, Speedy. Let me have this."

I went totally still. Did Aeron and I know each other before? He wanted me to remember for way more reasons than just going to kill the president with him. Was I supposed to be remembering him? Why was he such a dick to me if he was so affectionate when he was drunk?

He had me crushed to his chest, and he was snoring in an instant. Why didn't he do this the night I had a nightmare?

Was I supposed to be remembering Aeron this entire time?

Fourteen

I didn't have any memory nightmares that night. When I woke up, Aeron was nowhere to be found. I looked out the front door, and I didn't see him or his horse. I found him outside in the backyard cooking over a makeshift stove. He didn't seem hungover at all. He must have super drunk powers because I didn't get as drunk as he did, and he wasn't paying for it today.

He was back to being a cold fish.

"Hey, Ariel. One of the best things about Gabriel's Haven is that they have chickens. Someone left eggs on the front porch. It's not much, but I scrambled them with some rosemary that grows in the yard."

"It's a hot meal, and I'm grateful for whatever you can cook. I know it's not always going to be like this. What did you do for this town that they like you so much? I know you didn't bribe them with chocolate."

"I came through here looking to map a safe route from Washington State to Mexico. When I got to the gate, Scooter and his gang were here, causing trouble. I caused them a little trouble. I guess you could say I made them dead."

I just nodded and took the plate from him.

"Because your specialty is death, right?"

"Exactly."

"Are you ever going to explain what that means?"

"Not any time soon, Speedy."

"Why do you sometimes call me Speedy and sometimes Ariel?

Aeron just shrugged and wouldn't look at me.

"Sometimes, I slip up."

If he would not mention last night, should I? Would it make shit weird? Shit was already pretty weird. I already had him talking a little, and he let his hair down and got drunk with me last night. I decided not to let shit get any weirder and just enjoy my eggs.

"What's the plan for today?"

"Cougar wants to meet with us, and then we are headed out."

"We aren't leaving as early as before."

"No, because we aren't in dangerous territory, and we aren't going through it. Most of the way to the next stop is abandoned except for Rage Heads, and they aren't bad. They are mostly half-starved and weak out that way. The closer we get to Los Angeles, the worse it will get."

"How is Los Angeles?"

"California isn't doing so bad. We will have to be careful about getting to your apartment."

"Um, what is your horse going to do in Los Angeles?"

Aeron smirked at me.

"Why are you so concerned with Meremoth?"

"That's not a normal horse!"

"Maybe, maybe not."

"Asshole," I muttered.

"You know you love me."

"Excuse me?"

Aeron waved his fork at me.

"You just wait."

Wait for what? My memories to come back? He certainly wasn't helping with that. Could he help with that? If my mind would break if my memories were triggered wrong, this was all up to me. Maybe I could make a game of it. Perhaps I could find a way to trick Aeron into answering my questions that I could find out about him without triggering memories.

"Did we know each other before?"

"Why do you ask that?"

"Because you wouldn't have had my blue bat if you weren't looking for me. You knew where I lived, and you went to my apartment to get things for me. Why would you do all that, and how do you know all this shit about me if we didn't know each other before?"

"That's a story for another day. We need to talk to Cougar and get on the road. It's a long way to Los Angeles, and I'm hoping your apartment triggers some memories for you."

That was a story for right now. How was answering me if we knew each other in the past going to hurt me? I was getting sick of Aeron's shit. I stomped out the front door after him. We argued all the way through the town. Aeron kept snapping at me to keep my voice down and drop it. I wasn't having any of that. It was frustrating not remembering your entire life. Aeron had all the answers, and he wouldn't even give me hints.

We were still arguing when Aeron knocked on a house

with a large door. Cougar opened the door and cocked an eyebrow at us.

"If you need this one, you might want to keep her happy because she looks like she wants to rip your balls off."

"She does," I growled.

"Get in here and let's talk this out like adults."

I followed her to a beautiful living room and sat on the couch as far away from Aeron as I could. He refused to look at me and scowled at the wall. It was like the way he was when he was drunk never happened.

"Now, what are you fighting about?"

Aeron and I both started talking at once.

"He's keeping secrets from me."

"She's being ridiculous. I'm trying to keep her safe, and she fights me at every turn."

Cougar held up her hand.

"Ariel, why do you think he's keeping secrets?"

I couldn't help it. I fell out laughing. Why did I *think* he was keeping secrets? He even lied about not having a last name.

"I woke up in a hospital with no memories. I didn't even know my own name. The only living person in the hospital was this asshole, and he hands me a Smurf blue baseball bat and expects me to remember something. He was at that hospital for a reason, or he wouldn't have had my old bat and my clothes from my apartment. He even lied about not having a last name!"

"I get why you're upset, Ariel. I do. But it's the end of the world. Does it really matter if you know his last name? Cougar is not my real name. It's what I prefer to be called now."

"What if he's keeping his last name from me because he knows it'll make me remember him?"

Cougar sighed.

"Ariel, I met Aeron before the war broke out. He warned us about the water then, and he let us know that they were about to drop bombs. Even back then, Aeron was working with a team trying to end this. He was trying to put all the pieces together, and there were things he needed to find. How do you know his entire team didn't spend years gathering a file on you, and you are a piece to this puzzle?"

I threw up my hands and wanted to shriek in frustration.

"Try asking him that! He won't answer either way."

"Aeron? Care to chime in?"

"You know I hate it when you mediate me, right? Neither of you understands. The way Ariel's memories were taken from her wasn't natural. The person who took them didn't want her to ever remember. They didn't want her ever to be found either. That research facility was like Fort Knox with security. I suspect one of the doctors or nurses got a bite outside and said nothing. They came to work like everything was normal and turned on their shift.

"That's the only reason I was able to get in that facility. It was safer to fight my way through a bunch of Rage Heads than get through the security they had in place. Do you get that? You weren't supposed to wake up, Speedy. And if you did, they put precautions in place in case anyone tried to help you remember. I can't tell you a fucking thing because of what they did to you at that facility. Cut me some slack. I want you to remember just as much as you do."

I just sat there with my mouth gaping open. Who the

fuck did that to me, and were they still alive? Smurfette would like to meet them. *Why* would anyone do that to me? I didn't remember much, but what I knew of myself was that I was an artist who played on a recreational softball team and liked to attend concerts. And I was totally fucked because he couldn't tell me why.

"I don't remember much, but I remember a little. Why would anyone bother?"

"Now, Ariel," Cougar said, resting her elbows on her knees. "I know how frustrating this is for you, but can you understand that it's frustrating for Aeron too? You are clearly crucial if someone went to such lengths to take you out of the equation, and it would help all of us if Aeron could just tell you everything.

"None of this is fair. If it were up to me, I'd be living in a house with electricity and access to a grocery store teaching kindergarten again. I don't know why you are important either, just that you are. I don't want Aeron to tell you anything either because we need you functioning for whatever his plan is. Can you be patient?"

Did I have a choice? I didn't ask for this, but if the end of the world was happening and I was somehow important, then I just needed to nut up and deal with it. I'd have to stop giving Aeron a hard time.

"I guess."

I'd be patient, but it didn't mean I had to like it.

"Good. And you, Aeron. You have a bad temper, and you can be rough around the edges. I know you are frustrated she can't remember, but imagine how she feels. She's desperate for anything to hold on to."

Aeron crossed his arms and grumped.

"I guess."

"Good. Now, both of you be nicer to each other, and

you might just complete your mission. Do you need anything for the road? We found a huge stash of MREs when we found your booze. I can send you with a few."

"Anything you can spare would be great. We found a supply closet, and that was where I found your chocolate, but I'd like to ride straight on with as minimal stops as possible. We will be sleeping rough along the way. Some cities along our route are overrun with Rage Heads, and our options for sleeping are as safe as I could make them."

Cougar narrowed her eyes at Aeron.

"If you went through so much trouble to find this girl and you keep pissing her off, then make them safer. If she's a piece of your puzzle, then you do better at making things safe."

"Yes, ma'am. We do need to be headed out soon."

"Then, come pick out some MREs and get on your way. I mean it, Aeron. If harm comes to this girl, you will have all of Gabriel's Haven after your ass."

Fifteen

Aeron refused to talk to me for the rest of the day. It was pretty fucking miserable, considering we were sharing a horse. It made the lengthy ride even longer. Sometimes, he rode Meremoth hard and fast, and sometimes, we just walked. I honestly had no idea where we were. Most of the street signs were either totally obliterated by one of the bombs, or someone had spray-painted over it.

It wasn't chaos and anarchy with the vandalism. Someone tried to warn people before they left that city. There were dire warnings on most of the street signs about zombies and Rage Heads. I guess I took comfort that at least one person in those towns got out to spray paint those warnings. I wondered if they were still alive. Did they find a city like Gabriel's Haven to call home, or did they meet up with someone like Scooter's gang?

Aeron shushed me like a noisy toddler when I tried to ask. I guess he was mad Cougar had to give him a spanking, and now he was pouting about it. I was pissed about what she said to us too, but for different reasons than Aeron probably was. I knew something had been done to me now, and I was somehow important, but I had no way of asking because of what they had done to make me forget. It was infuriating.

Aeron's hand tensed on my waist, and he finally decided I was worthy of talking to.

"We have to stop for the night. We are about to enter a Rage Head infested city. No living soul exists here except them, so they will be starving. Do exactly what I say when we pass the motel sign that just says *Dead Inside*. We are sleeping in an abandoned train car. I know it's not the Ritz Carlton, and there's no running water, but it's the safest place for us."

"I'm not complaining about roughing it, Aeron."

Aeron let out this little growl.

"I am. You deserve a bed and running water, Ariel. This is the best I can do tonight."

Sometimes, Aeron said the littlest things and were so sweet. The other times, he was shushing me, and I wanted to punch him in the nuts.

"Aeron, it's not your fault we are sleeping in a train car tonight. It's not like there are any other options."

"Get your bat ready and be on alert. The Rage Heads here usually congregate towards the downtown area. We'll cut through the woods to get to the train, but there could be a stray Rage Head who has gotten a taste for wildlife. I will have to bring Meremoth close so we can kill it. We don't want it to signal the others. If we wake up in that train car surrounded by Rage Heads, it will be next to impossible to get away. Believe me, that happened to me the last time I was on my way up here."

"Got it."

"Teamwork, Speedy. I drive Meremoth. You kill the Rage Heads with Smurfette."

Aeron had a *lot* of faith in my zombie killing abilities, which just opened up a million questions I would never get the answer to. I gave Smurfette a twirl as Meremoth broke through the trees. I could do this. I was on a huge, demonic horse that ran faster than anything I'd seen before, and they were rotting corpses. I could bash a bitch's head in from up here.

I could see three of them up ahead milling about in the trees. Aeron spurred Meremoth, and we took off towards the closest one. I knew I could hit a fastpitch softball. I held Smurfette with one hand as we went racing towards this rotting Rage Head. Meremoth raced by, and I swung away. I felt its head crack under my bat. I let out this maniacal laugh. I probably shouldn't be having so much fun with this, but there were only three of them, and it was like horseback zombie polo.

The one to our right let out that shriek they made when they were calling their kind. It was a little less fun when ten more of them broke through the trees and started racing towards us. Was I insane that I thought this was a good time when there were only three of them? I probably was.

Now, Aeron was the one laughing like a maniac.

"You asked me if this was a normal horse. Let me show you what Meremoth can do, Speedy!"

Meremoth let out a snort, and I swear I saw steam come out his nose. Meremoth just decided to go zombie bowling. He plowed through the crowd of zombies and just started trampling skulls with his hooves. I was holding onto the pommel and swearing up a storm. If this crazy horse threw me into a crowd of Rage Heads because it was showing off, I would be upset.

Aeron grabbed my waist in a death grip.

"Hold on, Speedy!"

When you were on top of a horse in the middle of a murder rampage, and its handler told you to hang on, grab anything. These brainless Rage Heads didn't have a care that the horse was on a killing spree and just crushed several of their friend's heads. They just wanted to eat us. They came at us again. I shrieked and flung myself forward when this fucking horse reared back on two legs like it would fight these zombies like a boxer.

Okay, this was definitely *not* a normal horse. This was some sort of zombie killing murder horse. And he was my ride to Mexico. Maybe when we meet Aeron's friend Leif in Mexico, he'll have a nice bicycle I could ride on the handlebars.

I had all this bravado about taking out these zombies with Smurfette, but when the horse started murdering the dead, it all went out the window. I had thrown myself over Meremoth's neck, clutching his mane. There were two Rage Heads left, and they were coming right at us, but I was shaking so badly I wasn't sure I could fight them.

Aeron managed to produce his sword from nowhere again. *Where did he keep that thing?* He beheaded both of them and chuckled. He pat me on the back.

"You okay, Speedy?"

"That is *not* a normal horse. You've got some devil killer horse."

"Not a devil horse, Speedy, but he is a fighter. We will probably have to fight off a few more on our way to the train. You can't freak out when Meremoth fights. He won't throw you, and you are perfectly safe with me behind you."

A killer horse and a guy with secrets who could pull a sword out of nowhere. Yeah, I was totally safe.

Sixteen

I got my shit together for the rest of the ride to the train. If I was the one killing the zombies, then I didn't have to worry about crazy horses throwing me off. I needed to be focused. I guess Aeron got a cue I didn't like it when his horse helped out because he kept that mysterious sword out and we killed our way through the woods as a team. Let's do more of that and less letting the horse out to play when I'm sitting on its back.

Meremoth brought us straight up to a train car. This wasn't a passenger train. It was some sort of cargo train. If this place was swarming with Rage Heads and Aeron got surrounded when he slept in this car once, how was the horse still alive? Would he at least tell me that?

Aeron flung the door open, and we climbed inside. It looked like Aeron had spent a lot of time preparing this car. The crates were stacked in such a way that it would make an additional barrier to the steel door for anything that wanted to get inside.

He'd made this cozy little nest in the middle of the crates. He must have been looking for me or brought someone else here because there were two sleeping bags rolled out and a bucket at the very end of the car if we needed to go to the bathroom. I could see a case of bottled water stashed in the corner.

"This is great, Aeron."

"It's sleeping bags in an abandoned train car."

"Learn to take a compliment, dickhead. It's the apocalypse. We will not have houses every night."

"You deserve a house every night," Aeron muttered. I don't think he intended on me hearing that, but there were great acoustics in an abandoned train.

"Aeron? Are you finally going to tell me the deal with your horse? It kills for you, and if you got swarmed when you slept here, why didn't they eat the horse?"

"I'll tell you this, Ariel. There are only four horses like Meremoth in the entire world. Meremoth and his three brothers are the only horses of their kind. That is why you think he's not a normal horse."

That made sense, but other things didn't.

"How do you make your sword just appear like that?"

"Help me move these crates. We have to secure this place before we can sleep here."

I hated it when he did that, but I also didn't want to get eaten alive, so I helped him move the crates to make a barrier around us. Aeron just pretended like I never asked him about his sword as he plopped down with his rucksack.

"How do you feel about Cheetos and chicken soup for dinner? I've got some creamed corn, but I don't know who actually likes that stuff."

"What are you going to eat?"

"I've got ten more bags of Funyuns left. I would take the vegetable beef soup, unless you want it?"

"Cheetos and chicken soup sound great."

"It's cold, and we must eat it from the can."

"Aeron? I know. I won't complain."

I was actually starving, but I'd never tell Aeron that. We had eggs for breakfast, and we only ate chips and water on our brief stop for lunch. I'd never tell Aeron that, and I'd be grateful for any food we had. There was no point in complaining about being hungry when the shit had gotten so bad outside. I knew Aeron was just as hungry as I was.

We didn't have any spoons. I ripped the pop-top off the can and just drank from it. I'd worry about bad manners later. I slurped up that cold can of soup like it was my last meal, then mowed my way through the Cheetos. I grabbed a bottle of water from the stash in the corner to wash it all down.

I wouldn't mind washing in a river. I was pretty sure I was ripe at this point, but what else was I going to do? I could stink, or I could get eaten.

Aeron gathered the trash and stuck it in a corner. It was getting dark in the train car, and I was having difficulty seeing. I had no idea what all those bombs did to the atmosphere, but the weather had gotten weird. It was always sweltering hot during the day and so humid, it was like walking around in soup. When the sun went down, the temperature always dropped drastically.

"We should get some sleep, Ariel. We have a better chance of avoiding the Rage Heads if we start early. The Rage Heads don't sleep, but they go into a sort of a trance at night. It's usually broken once the sun comes up. I learned that one the hard way."

"Good night, Aeron," I said, crawling into my sleeping bag.

I was about to wonder if I would have any more dream memories when Aeron pressed himself against my back and flung his leg and arm over me. What the fuck? He wasn't drunk this time.

"Aeron? What are you doing?"

"Shut up. It gets cold in these cars at night, and you'll get sick."

"Don't tell me to shut up. You always act like you're repulsed when you have to touch me. Now, you want to snuggle?"

"I'm keeping you warm. That's all."

Keeping me warm, my ass. This was the second time he held me like this while we slept, and he had his face buried in my neck like he was enjoying this. I could feel something pressing into my back like he was definitely enjoying this.

Was it fucked up that I liked it too? There was so much about Aeron I didn't know, and I wasn't all that sure I could trust him with that crazy horse, his mysterious sword, and all his secrets. But it was nice to be held. I felt safe like this. How fucked up. I wasn't sure if I could trust Aeron and his plot to kill the president, but I felt totally safe with him holding me at night.

And I wanted him to do it again. We fought all the time, and we just had a kindergarten teacher try to mediate for us, but this just worked.

I'd fight with him until I found out the truth, but I wouldn't mind sleeping like this every night.

SEVENTEEN

I don't know how I slept through this. I woke up when Aeron started shaking me. I bolted awake and heard the sound of wails and hundreds of fingernails scrabbling against the side of the car. How did we both sleep through this?

"We're surrounded, Ariel. I have a plan. Can you run and carry a bag? If we leave these behind, we will be without food and water, and we must make a supply run. Most of the stores from here to the next stop are picked dry, and we *have* to have water."

I felt my heart beating in my throat. Shit just got real. I could hear them out there. It sounded like there were hundreds of them surrounding all sides of our car. How were we going to get out of this?

"I can carry whatever the fuck you want me to if you get us out of here."

"Good. Grab that bag and follow me."

I grabbed the bag, and I would do whatever the fuck he wanted me to as long as I didn't get eaten. Aeron put his finger over this lip like he wanted me to be quiet. He pointed upwards towards the roof, and I saw a hatch up at the top. He pulled some crates over so he could climb up and get the hatch open.

"Come here. I'll give you a boost and throw the bags up."

Aeron was a lot gentler with me as he gave me a boost through the hatch. I was not prepared for what I saw when I climbed on the roof of the car. I think every single zombie in this town was surrounding us, and they all wanted to eat us alive. They were wailing, and the sounds of their nails against the car were like nails on a chalkboard.

Aeron tossed the bags up, and I pulled them next to me. Aeron hauled himself to the roof of the car. He saw the look I was giving him. I'd never seen this many Rage Heads in one place before. I don't think we even brought this many down on Scooter's gang. Aeron pulled me into a massive hug like he was a huggy person. It surprised me, but I really needed a hug right now.

"Follow me, and I'll get you out of this alive, Ariel."

I didn't know much about Aeron. I had a bunch of weird theories about him and his horse, but there was one fact about Aeron I knew. He always kept me safe. Aeron could get us out of this or die trying.

"I know, Aeron."

"This is the plan. We will run along the top of the roofs and jump across until we get to the caboose. Meremoth will wait for us."

"Won't they chase us?"

Aeron whipped off his shirt. I had no idea why, but I got an eyeful.

"They hunt by smell and sound. I'm giving us a head start."

Aeron pulled a pocket knife from his back pocket and sliced his forearm. He rubbed his blood all over the shirt and tossed it into the rabid herd of Rage Heads.

"Run, now!" he hissed.

We took off running, flying over train cars. A few Rage Heads followed us, but most of them were still fighting over his bloody shirt. Don't ask me how that horse got the memo to be waiting by the caboose, but there he was, just like Aeron said he would be.

I wasn't even going to ask or question that fucking horse at the moment. I was just grateful it could magically appear where needed. I followed Aeron down the ladder clutching Smurfette. Aeron was on the back of the car, killing the Rage Heads that followed us.

I felt fingers brush my ankle. Oh, fuck no. I didn't just run across the roof of a train just to die at the end. I let go of the ladder with one hand and bashed its brains in. I hopped on the platform and joined Aeron.

Aeron practically threw me on Meremoth and jumped on behind me. He spurred the horse, and we took off running. We didn't stop until we got to a road sign covered in graffiti. Meremoth abruptly stopped, and Aeron jumped down. He practically yanked me out of the saddle and started examining me.

"Are you okay? Were you hurt at all?"

"Aeron, I'm fine. I'm not hurt."

Aeron was holding my cheeks, and his gray eyes bored into mine. There was this look on his face like he didn't know what to do next.

"Fuck it," he growled.

Aeron pulled me to his chest and crushed his lips to mine. I didn't fight it. It was weird. I kissed him back with just as much passion as he kissed me, and I loved every minute of it.

That's when I remembered him. I hadn't met Aeron in person before. I couldn't remember what we talked about, but I knew Aeron from a chatroom. He was my friend, and we were close. I talked to his team too. Well, I talked to Leif. I couldn't remember talking to the other two people on his team.

We were all friends. I liked them, and they liked me. But what the fuck did we talk about? Was I plotting to kill the president when someone kidnapped me and took me to that facility so they could wipe my memories?

I touched Aeron's cheek.

"We met in a chatroom."

Aeron beamed at me and kissed me so hard, my knees went weak.

"Yes! What else do you remember?"

I shook my head. I wanted to give him something, anything, that I remembered more about him than just a chatroom. I didn't even know what we talked about.

"Just that we met there. There were three of us in the room. I knew your team before all this. I can't remember your usernames, but I know you told me your real names at one point. I don't know what we talked about. How did I meet you and Leif, but not the other two?"

Aeron kissed my forehead and stroked my hair.

"It's a start. If I had known kissing you would have brought something back, I would have done it way before now. Keeping you at a distance was so hard. I couldn't deal with it anymore. I could have lost you back there if my plan didn't work."

"Aeron, if we had some online thing before, why were you acting like a dick to me before those zombies almost ate us? You were acting like just touching me grossed you out."

"Let's get back on the road. It's not safe to stay here, and we need to reach our next stop. I'll explain, I promise."

This time, when Aeron put me on the back of his horse, it was like I was breakable. He climbed up behind me, and it was a lot more intimate when he wrapped his arm around my waist and rested it on my thigh. I didn't speak when we started moving. I didn't want to ruin whatever this was.

"It was my fault you got taken, Speedy. We were all talking in the chatroom and planning. You were just supposed to disappear one day and meet us in Mexico. I was the one that didn't want it to play out like that. I was the one that insisted on crossing the border to get you. I brought attention to you. You were supposed to meet me at your favorite restaurant. We would eat, and then I would take you back with me.

"When I got to the restaurant, your car was there, but you were nowhere to be found. I searched everywhere and tried calling you. Your cell phone had already been disconnected. I didn't think you had changed your mind or your car wouldn't have been there. I went to your apartment, and the door was ajar. Someone had gone through your apartment looking for anything you might have left behind on the way out.

"You didn't meet Dice and Asher because they weren't on the team yet. We really could have used their help to find you. You just disappeared the day we were supposed to meet, and there were no clues in your apartment. The day after you disappeared, the first signs of the rage mutation started showing up."

"How does an artist and softball player factor into any of this shit?"

"I swear, when the time is right, I'll explain everything. We're making progress, Speedy. The more you remember, the more I can tell you."

I smiled to myself.

"Since you're in a sharing mood, Meremoth is not a normal horse, is he?"

Aeron chuckled.

"No, he's not, but that's a story for another time."

I knew it.

Eighteen

The change in Aeron was pretty fucking drastic. He was still locked up tight when he came to telling me anything about him, and he was still acting like he didn't have a last name. He wasn't telling me anything about my past, and I got that part. I totally did. I got that it was the apocalypse and people were renaming themselves, but maybe it would trigger something if he would just tell me more about himself. I still had no idea what we talked about in that chatroom.

Still, even though there were things that were a big nope with him when it came to a discussion, Aeron had become a chatty bastard since that kiss. He was pointing out things on our ride and explaining my surroundings instead of taking me on a ride through the unfamiliar and leaving me to figure it out.

I could just make out something in the distance. It looked like a broken-down car and a woman holding what looked like a baby on the side of the road.

"Look, Aeron. I think there's someone in trouble up ahead."

Aeron's hand tightened on my waist.

"No, we're the ones in trouble. That's not a helpless woman on the side of the road with a broken-down car. She's the bait, and she's holding a weapon in those rags disguised as a baby. Her gang is probably in the bushes waiting to ambush us."

What a cynical fuck.

"How do you know?"

"People don't survive on their own anymore. Rage Heads outnumber humans, and if you don't have someone at your back, some living are even worse than the dead. The only way to survive now is to align yourself with a gang or community. She would be dead or a Rage Head now if it were just her and a baby."

"You're not part of a gang," I pointed out.

"No, but I know who the gangs are, and I've made allies with communities all over the country. I help them, and they help me. Gabriel's Haven is not the only place they have given me a home."

"Maybe her community needs help."

"More like her gang saw a man and a woman on a horse and wanted to steal the horse. I know most of the gangs, but I don't know all of them. Humanity has gone to shit, Speedy. These people will kill us for our supplies and Meremoth, and that's not the worst thing they could do."

"I believe you, Aeron. So, what do we do? Go around them?"

"No, indeed. The successful gangs have booby-trapped the surrounding woods to cut down on the Rage Head population. That was another reason I went straight through Scooter's territory instead of around."

"Booby traps. It's the fucking apocalypse; of course, there are booby traps. So, what exactly do we do?"

"Remember when you asked me if Meremoth was a normal horse?"

"Yes, and you said he wasn't. You won't tell me what he is, just that there are only four like him."

"Do you trust me?"

"Are you about to do crazy shit where the horse starts murdering things, and I'm scared I will die?"

"You'll never die when you're riding Meremoth, Speedy. Meremoth will get us past that little trap alive."

"Okay, then. Do it."

"Yippee-ki-yay, motherfucker!" Aeron yelled loud enough for everyone to hear.

The woman ran to the center of the road and started frantically waving at us. I knew I should have recognized Aeron's line from somewhere, but I couldn't remember shit. As soon as he finished, Meremoth took off running. If I thought that horse ran fast before, that was *nothing* compared to what he was doing now. I flung myself across his neck as my surroundings became a blur.

We were headed straight for the woman in the middle of the road. I wondered what was going through her head as a petrified woman clutching a blue baseball bat and an insane man waving a sword and screaming like a cowboy came barreling at her at this pace. Was she going to move? Because I already knew Meremoth had no intention of stopping.

Aeron was right. She was the bait, and we were the prey. Her gang saw we had every intention of running her over with this huge horse going impossibly fast and started spilling into the street screaming at us. Most of them had knives, and I saw some machetes, but only a few of them had guns. I didn't have to speak to know they didn't want to waste ammo on us. They would have used the guns to threaten us, then killed us with one of their sharp things.

One of the men tackled the woman as we flew by them. Someone took a shot at us, but Meremoth was running so fucking fast, they were soon long past us. Meremoth slowed to a trot, and Aeron was laughing like a crazy person. He patted Meremoth's neck fondly while I was still draped across it shaking like a leaf.

"He loves it when I let him do that."

"I think you enjoyed that too, you crazy son of a bitch."

"There's nothing quite like riding Meremoth when he's totally unleashed."

"You're insane," I hissed.

"And you're still alive, Speedy."

Well, fuck. He had me there.

Nineteen

The rest of our ride out of Washington State was pretty uneventful with Aeron as my guide. He had the apocalypse nailed down to a T. Our route was carefully planned for the most part. Aside from the town he found me in, we didn't stop in any significant nasty gang territory, and when we stopped in a Rage Head infested town to sleep, Aeron had his own booby traps to keep us safe.

We had to make more supply runs as our stash from the supply closet was running low, but we worked well as a team. We didn't luck into any more undiscovered closets, and we only snatched mystery cans after that. Aeron said the supplement hadn't been added to the water supply in a long time, but it still wasn't safe to risk taking a shower in some places we stopped at that still had running water.

Taking a shower became this huge luxury, even if the water was cold. I had precisely three pairs of panties to last me for the entire apocalypse, and I don't even want to talk about how long I had to wear a pair before I got to wash them again. I had long abandoned the bra Aeron grabbed for me. It was the apocalypse, and I was saying I didn't have to wear that awful thing.

As for Aeron, as much as I thought he was an asshole before, I liked him now. I could see why I made friends with him in that chatroom and agreed to follow him to Mexico. I still had no idea *why* I was disappearing to Mexico, but I could see why I liked the guy.

My memories were still coming in pieces, and they weren't really pieces I could use. I knew that before all of this, I worked as a tattoo artist in this little shop in Los Angeles. My shop only did custom work, and some of my art won awards at tattoo conventions. I still had no idea why a tattoo artist was so crucial to the apocalypse.

My nightmare dreams were still coming. The man from my dreams who left me at the lab played a prominent role, but I could never see his face in my nightmares. I could tell that I loved him in the first dream, and I didn't want him to leave me at that lab.

As much as my four-year-old self loved him in that dream, whenever he showed up in my dreams, I knew deep down that I hated this man. Aeron said the man was my father. All he would tell me about this man was that I grew up in New York and confirmed I hated him. Aeron said I ran away from him when I was fifteen. I ran as far as I could get. I hopped on a bus to California and had myself legally emancipated when I was sixteen.

I could feel it even now when I thought about my dreams. I *loathed* my father. Aeron wouldn't confirm or deny, but I knew he wasn't dead. He was pure evil if he let those people do those things to me as a child. He was probably alive and kicking. Evil people were like cockroaches and difficult to kill. He probably has his own gang like Scooter did and was raping and eating people. I couldn't remember much about him, but I just got this vibe based on what I could remember that he'd resort to that and not feel bad about it at all.

Aeron looked so relieved when I remembered something. I think he wanted me to remember more than I did, and I wanted my memories back more than anything. He would get so excited and try to fill in what he could. He would start talking, then realize he might tell me too much and clam up.

Apparently, my memory loss was like Meremoth. It shouldn't have been possible, and I'd never heard of anything like it before. All Aeron would confirm was that it wasn't natural, and I wasn't ready to hear it yet. My working theory was that someone had cross-bred a horse with some sort of weird DNA and created some kind of super horse like Meremoth. I was pretty sure someone brainwashed me before they put me in a coma, so I wouldn't remember. Why Aeron couldn't tell me that, I had no idea.

I breathed a sigh of relief when I saw the *Welcome to California* sign. Aeron said I was born in New York, but it felt like I was coming home. Sure, the sign had been vandalized, but I was back. Aeron pointed to one of the symbols on the sign. It was a bloody eye.

"The Forsaken run California now. It's a tight run ship. They've got people in every city. They've granted me access to the border, but we must present you as we did in Gabriel's Haven. I know California is your home, but shit has changed. They don't let anyone in that hasn't been vetted now. California is one of the remaining states that survived, and it's all because people came together to make it so. They have some pretty harsh policies here. If you aren't contributing or you cause trouble, they banish you. They put a bag over your head, drive you out a way, and just leave you."

"Remind me not to piss them off."

"Just follow the rules. Don't steal, don't kill, and if they give you a job, do it without complaint. Everyone pitches in, and they look down on taking more than what you are given."

Meremoth approached a wall that was similar to the one around Gabriel's Haven. This one was even bigger. Did they build a wall around California? Just like Gabriel's Haven, we were greeted by guns first. A head popped over and glared at us. Aeron wasn't recognized on sight this time.

"What do you want?"

Aeron reached in his bag and pulled a white cloth with a red eye painted on it.

"I've been given access, but she hasn't. She's from Los Angeles. We are just passing through. We are hoping to stop by her old apartment, and then we will be on our way."

"Supposing her apartment is now occupied. They might not want her in there, and we don't like violence."

"It's not occupied. I worked that out directly with Jade."

"Ooh, fancy. How do we know your friend doesn't intend to cause trouble?"

"I'll vouch for her. You can call Jade, and she'll vouch for me. As I said, we are only passing through. We don't intend to stay. I just need to get her to her old apartment."

The man at the gate whipped out a satellite phone. I guess to call this mysterious Jade. Did Aeron have a satellite phone to call his team? I'd never seen him with one this entire time, but he said he'd spoken with them. Why would he hide a phone from me? Who was I going to call, anyway?

The man at the gate wrapped up his conversation, but he still looked at us like he trusted us about as far as he could throw us.

"Jade vouches for you. She says if your friend acts up, you're banished."

The gate swung open, and Meremoth took us through. California wasn't like what I could barely remember. Bombs wholly destroyed some buildings. It looked like they were coming together and slowly rebuilding, but it was a process. I remembered the city I woke up in. All the grass was dead, and the landscape seemed barren. It looked like they were trying to change this because I could see some green peeking through all the brown.

Aeron told me gangs overran Los Angeles, but it sounded like just one gang, and they were doing their best to keep California running. There was almost no litter on the street like there was everyplace else we went, and if there had been broken glass, it was already cleaned up.

I could see some people were using cars, but most people on the street were using bicycles or rollerblades. I didn't see a single person on horseback like we were, and Aeron's crazy horse got some strange looks because that thing was enormous. I think Aeron enjoyed getting stared at, and so did the horse. I swear that fucking horse was preening under all the stare.

We were still a long way away from Los Angeles. I had no idea where we would sleep until Aeron pulled the horse up in front of a hotel. You could get a hotel room in

California during the apocalypse? What the ever-loving fuck?

Aeron didn't stop at the front desk. He led me straight down the hallway to a room. He pulled a keyring out of his pocket and unlocked the door.

"Um, Aeron? Why do you have a hotel room?"

"It was one of the first things the Forsaken started rebuilding when they took over. A lot of the living lost their homes, or the living conditions were so bad they couldn't stay there. There aren't enough skilled people to rebuild that many houses at once, so they focused on the hotels first. They gave the displaced rooms while they started on the houses. They are trying to do as many things as solar as they can, like this hotel. Be grateful we've got power while we are in California. You can take a hot shower."

"And wash my clothes. I'll bet I reek to high heaven right now."

"I like your smell."

"If that's your way of flirting, my stink is not the way to my heart."

"Go shower and wash your thongs. I'll see if I can scrounge up something better than mystery cans for dinner."

I didn't care if it was hot. I hadn't showered in four days, and I didn't want to talk about how long I'd been wearing my last clean pair of panties. I went running towards the shower like I was dying of thirst in the desert. Who knew when I would get to shower again?

TWENTY

I'll say this for the Forsaken. They were running California pretty smoothly, given everything that was going on. Aeron was able to negotiate no one getting assigned my old apartment and getting hotel rooms in all the cities he had asked for in exchange for the advice he had given Jade, the leader of the Forsaken. Aeron was spreading the word about the bottled water among the survivors. He told me Leif thought people with AB negative blood were somehow immune to the mutations that the supplement caused, but he hadn't been able to study prolonged exposure to it among AB negative people.

I had to ask about Jade. She was running a pretty tight ship here. What they had built in California was nothing short of amazing.

"Jade? That was her stage name. She used to be an exotic dancer, and she saw some shit before all this went down. She's a little badass. She's probably ninety pounds soaking wet, and all of California fears her. She's a pussycat if she likes you."

I let out this little growl. Was I jealous of Jade? Did I even have any right to be? Aeron and I only knew each other online before. We'd only kissed once this entire time and snuggled when we slept. I had zero claims over him, but it seriously bothered me that while I was in a coma, he possibly flirted with this woman to get all these perks in California.

Aeron just smirked at me like he could read me like an open book. He was totally getting off on this. I wanted to punch that smile right off his cute, arrogant face.

"Jade is a lesbian, Speedy. She'd probably cut my balls off with a rusty knife if I even hinted at having sex with her. And I don't want to have sex with her. You're cute when you're jealous."

"Shut up," I said, throwing the pillow at his face.

"No, seriously. The greatest shortstop of girl's fast-pitch softball on the West Coast is jealous over little old me. A guy could get an ego."

"I think you had a fat head way before we met in that chatroom."

Aeron threw the pillow back at me.

"Yeah, I totally did. I will hit the shower. Answer the door when there's a knock. It's dinner."

Room service during the fucking apocalypse? Why were we leaving California again? Couldn't we just hole up here instead of going to murder someone? Even if the president was the major shareholder of Armilus, how was killing him going to make any of this better? There were walking corpses and a desolate landscape. Canada and Mexico were no more and got swallowed by the United States. He was running all three now. What more could he possibly want?

Aeron had those answers, and I wasn't sure he would

tell me. I tried to focus on remembering. I needed to put together the pieces of what I remembered for a bigger picture. I had all these memories of a faceless father that I hated, but I never saw my mother once.

Big question. Why did I end up at two research facilities in my life? I knew the second time, it was to keep me hidden in a coma. Why not kill me if I was somehow involved in all this? What was the purpose of all the tests when I was a child, and why did they need me terrorized to do them?

I couldn't remember much about those tests to know how long they were done. All I could remember was the night I ran. I remembered that night in a dream back in Washington State. My adrenaline was pumping, and I had planned the entire thing. My father kept me locked in my bedroom at night. I could only ever leave the house to go to the exclusive all girl's private school he had me enrolled in, and I had to come straight home.

I spent two years planning my escape, but I made it to the bus station with the money I stole. I ran all the way to California and didn't stop looking over my shoulder for two years. Even after I became legally emancipated from him, it scared me he would kidnap me and bring me back.

The only person I could think of that would kidnap me from California and keep me in a coma during the apocalypse instead of killing me was him. If I would be killing the president with Aeron and his friends and someone found out, they would have just put a bullet in my head.

Those people that staffed the research facility and watched over me wouldn't have stayed if they weren't being given something in return. Someone probably went in with a Rage Head bite because they feared losing whatever perks were being offered for keeping me alive too.

My stomach sunk to my feet. I was important because my father was somehow involved in all this. I had a feeling all those tests that were done on me was to prepare for all of this.

Was my father now the President of the United States? Was that Aeron's big secret, and why he only ever referred to him as Isaiah? Was that why I was so important to all of this?

I knew I hated him. I could feel it in my bones. I wanted him dead, but how would killing him fix any of this?

TWENTY-ONE

I had every intention of demanding answers from Aeron when he got out the shower, and then he had to go and stroll out the bedroom, dripping wet, wearing nothing but a towel. I could see the defined V at his hips, and that towel looked like it would fall off at any minute. My throat went dry. Damn. He was one beautiful asshole. He had this grin on his face like he knew what I would ask and came out in that towel just to distract me.

I just blurted it out before I said something stupid or ripped that towel off and ran my tongue down that delicious V on his hips.

"Is my father the president, Aeron?"

"Did you have another memory?"

"No, but it's the only thing that makes sense."

Aeron sighed and sat on the foot of the bed.

"Yes, Ariel. Isaiah Nahum is your father. You might think you know how evil he is, but you have no idea."

"Did all those tests on me have anything to do with the supplement in the water that turned people into Rage Heads?"

Aeron refused to look at me.

"Are you sure you want the answer to that, Speedy?"

I really didn't. I didn't want to know one of those tests on me somehow paved the way for those corpses with red eyes who ate people. But I had to. I didn't have the option not to. I *had* to know how I fit into all of this.

"Yes, they do. Isaiah had been looking to create something like the Rage mutation for a long time."

I closed my eyes and braced myself.

"Did he succeed when he started testing on me?"

"Not right away. It had to be manipulated first."

I could feel tears welling up in my eyes, and I was trying not to let them fall.

"The AB negative people who ended up immune are because I'm AB negative, right?"

"Yes. But I can finally tell you this, Speedy. Your blood was used to create the Rage mutation. Leif has a theory he can take a blood sample from you to reverse it. If he can put it into a drone and release it into the air, the Rage Heads will all revert to corpses and drop dead on the spot.

"After we kill Isaiah, Asher will swoop in and get rid of the other dictators in power. We'll put the countries back to what they used to be. Asher can handle some more power-hungry militant gangs that like the status quo."

"How do you plan on doing all that with just the four of you? Why don't you start doing that now and rally the people to help you storm the White House?"

Aeron looked grim.

"Because the Rage mutation and World War III is not the worst thing Isaiah can do. It's just two parts of his plan. I can't explain just yet, Ariel, but it can get much worse than this."

He didn't need to paint me a picture. I couldn't imagine what could be worse than this. If Isaiah was planning something, based on what I could remember of him, I knew he could accomplish it.

I didn't know how Aeron intended to accomplish this with just the four of them. I just knew my father used my blood to create this mutation, and Leif might be able to use it to end this.

I was now totally on board with killing the President of the United States.

Twenty-Two

I didn't even get the chance to process the fact that something in my blood managed to animate corpses and turn them into cannibals. Someone knocked on the door. I didn't care who it was. I wanted Aeron to ignore it and continue this conversation. Like he would ever do that. If there was a way of getting out of explaining things to me, he would take it.

He jumped to his feet and nearly lost his towel.

"That's probably dinner. I know you want to keep talking, but we should take hot meals where we can get them. It's better than the mystery cans we've been eating, and we won't have to make any supply runs while we are in California. We can talk and eat. I promise."

Aeron was a lot of things, but he'd always kept his word when he made promises. I fell back on the pillow and waited for dinner. I ended up bolting back up when I heard the man in the room.

"Jade wants to see your friend when you pass through Sacramento. She has a request."

"Excuse me?"

"She saw your work at a convention. She says you won the top prize. She wants a tattoo."

"Does she know I don't remember how to give one?"

"She's aware. She says it's all muscle memory, and it will come back to you. She expects you both in Sacramento. She has the equipment. You just need to draw the art and tattoo her skin. I have your dinner. I hope it's to your liking."

I would have taken hot anything over the cold canned shit we had been eating, but what the fuck? I was supposed to tattoo the gang leader of California with no memories? I already knew if I fucked this up, we were both going to get banished from California. I was all on board with killing Isaiah and helping Aeron and his friends fix this, but I still wanted to come back and live here when this was over.

Based on how my life was going since I woke up from that coma, I would give a gang leader a shitty tattoo and get banished from California. Who wanted me to tattoo them in the middle of all this shit?

"It's fine. Tell her Speedy will be happy to do it," the traitorous bastard in a towel said.

Did he want to get us banned from California? Because that's how you get yourself banned from California. The man with our food disappeared, and as much as my empty stomach was growling, I had to ask Aeron what the fuck he was thinking.

"Aeron, I don't remember how to tattoo anyone! I'm not even sure I can draw a straight line."

"Jade doesn't take no for an answer, Speedy. Art is in your blood. You could draw with a blindfold on. In fact, I think if we could find a pencil and paper and just have you draw with your eyes closed, you might draw a memory.

Jade saw your work, and now she wants it permanently on her body. Doesn't that make you feel good a little? We will be banished if you don't do this."

"She will murder us if I permanently fuck up her body, Aeron."

"You won't, Ariel. I have this feeling it'll all work out. Don't you want to eat? I can hear your stomach from here."

Yeah, I was hungry, but could I have five minutes to lose my shit? I thought I was handling the end of the world pretty well so far, but that was because Aeron had this big plan, so I was following his lead. I had a healthy respect for the fact that I'd been in a coma since this started and had no idea what the fuck was going on. I was happy to let Aeron make all the decisions because so far, it had kept me alive.

What the fuck had my life been like before that someone I'd never met before knew who I was, knew I didn't remember shit, and wanted me to ink their skin permanently? Shit, was I famous before?

Aeron handed me a Tupperware container of food. It was still warm.

"A few things about California now. You can get take-out, but it's served in reusable containers, and they expect you to return them. It's not like anyone is getting paper or Styrofoam containers anymore. Almost all the food is vegetarian. You can still get eggs, but they are focusing on breeding farm animals for now. They only kill them for meat when they are too old to breed.

"A lot of farms got destroyed by bombs, so building up livestock with the animals that survived has been an ongoing process. When they do slaughter an animal, they use every part. People have learned to eat things like brains and tongues because sometimes, it's the only meat they can get."

I looked down at the Tupperware container in my hands.

"Is there mystery meat in here?"

"No, Speedy. People that could cook came together and started opening places to eat. They work with the farms, and they get provided grain, vegetables, and milk. You'd be amazed what they'd been able to do."

"I am amazed, Aeron! This place is amazing. That's why I don't want to get banished because I fucked Jade up."

"Forget the tattoo for tonight. Look what I got you."

Aeron looked like a little boy. He was giddy with excitement. I think he was more excited about what was in this Tupperware container than when we binge ate nachos. I might as well see what it was.

I pulled the lid off and resting on a bed of lettuce was falafel and tzatziki sauce. My mouth watered at the sight.

"You talked about this being your favorite food in the chatroom. It was right up there with Cheetos. When we were supposed to meet for me to take you to Mexico, you were supposed to show me the best falafel in Los Angeles. You ate it so much while you were chatting with us that Leif and I used to tease you about it."

I couldn't deal with Aeron. As much as I didn't like him at first, he ended up being so sweet. He could still be a grumpy fuck sometimes, but who manages to keep finding a girl's favorite food during the end of the world? The fact that he knew and kept trying was making my anxiety slip away about that tattoo I had to give.

Aeron went out of his way to do this for me, and I didn't want to spend tonight making him talk me down from some ledge. I decided just to chill. I needed to be kinder to Aeron because he was going above and beyond for me.

I leaned back against the pillows.

"What did you get?"

"Stuffed peppers and falafel. That tzatziki sauce is fresh from the farm. I got extra for both of us."

"Aeron? I'm sorry I gave you a hard time before. You're pretty great."

"No, I'm sorry, Ariel. I was so happy to find you that I wanted to kiss you right then and there, but you remembered nothing. I couldn't risk telling you anything because of your memories, and I couldn't touch you the way I wanted because I didn't want to run you off. It put me in a horrible mood, and you took the brunt of it."

"Truce?"

Aeron gave me this pained look. He wanted more than that. He wanted me to remember, and he wanted the same relationship we had in that chatroom. I couldn't give him that yet, but I could try.

"I know you can't tell me everything we talked about in that chatroom, but tell me insignificant things, like my falafel obsession. What are things that we talked about that were just us?"

Aeron gave me this sad smile.

"For starters, you got Leif and I hooked on this insane cartoon on YouTube. Someone released a new episode every week. You would rave about every episode and kept insisting we watch it at least once. Honestly, we kept putting it off because when you would talk about it, it sounds like something Oscar Wilde would have written on LSD. Finally, we got curious and watched it. We got hooked. We would discuss the latest episode in the chatroom when we weren't talking about your father."

"I was a falafel eating, cartoon watching, tattoo artist who named her baseball bat before all this?"

"You were an award-winning artist, Ariel. Your tattoos won at several conventions, and your paintings hung in galleries. You're allowed to be eccentric."

"What else did we talk about?"

"You were a huge flirt. You demanded photos from both Leif and I. You hit on both of us all the time. Leif can't wait to meet you too."

Well, didn't me before I lost my memories just open up a bunch of cans of shit? If Aeron kissed me out of the blue, was Leif going to do the same? My blood started this entire mess. Was some internet flirtation I had before all this going to fuck things up because Leif and Aeron decided they didn't want to work together anymore because I ruined their friendship?

"Aeron, I'm sorry if I led the two of you on. I don't want to break up your team because I teased both of you."

Aeron laughed in my face, and I had no idea what was so funny.

"Oh, Ariel. It was far more than just teasing. You were our online girlfriend, and we were both totally fine with that. We chatted in that room, but you also had our phone numbers. We texted and talked on the phone all the time."

Well, wasn't I just a kinky little minx before?

"So, we had this whole ménage thing going on online? How is that going to work once we are all together? I remember nothing about any of you. I'm growing fond of you now that I'm getting to know you, but I might not feel the same when I get my memories back."

"I know, Speedy. That's why I'm not trying to press you for anything."

"You're sitting there all hot and half-naked in the towel that keeps looking like it's about to fall off because you aren't pressing for anything?"

Aeron gave me this evil grin.

"I didn't say I would not show off. How is your dinner?"

"I could see myself raving about falafel in a chatroom. Have I told you how sweet you are for getting these for me?"

Aeron winked at me.

"I wouldn't mind hearing it again."

I already liked Aeron way more than I should. I apparently liked Leif too when I met him in that chatroom.

What the fuck would happen if we finally made it to Mexico?

TWENTY-THREE

I am in my bedroom in front of a computer. I am in my twenties, and I'm in a group chat for fastpitch softball. A stranger enters the room. I know everyone on most of the teams, and I know most of the fans who come to our games. I don't recognize this person. My stalker radar goes on high. I think every single girl on all the leagues has dealt with a deranged fan at one point. Girl's fastpitch softball caught on and had a rabid fan base.

This new user went by the name HorsemanD. He isn't focusing on one player, and he seems friendly. Still, my hackles are raised. My team all dealt with stalkers the same way, and we just had to put a man in his place because he wouldn't leave Pokey alone. This could all be some ruse. No one knew about this chatroom except my team and fans we trusted. How did this newbie find us?

I question him. He pretends to be new to the area and wants to see a game. That sets off even more red flags. The only way he could have found this room would be if he had already been to a game, and one of us on the team let him in on how to get here.

I wasn't standing for this. I wasn't letting another creep skeeze on my teammates. I click a few keys and get his IP address. I run a search. Why is someone in Mexico in our chatroom? I send him a private message demanding an answer.

"I'm not in California now, but I will be. I do want to see a game."

"Bullshit. The only way to find this room is because one of us gives it to you."

"Not if you are looking for it. Just like you dug around on me and found out I'm really in Mexico, I found your chatroom when I was looking for something like it."

"Why are you so interested in fastpitch softball, Tiger?"

"Are you this suspicious of everyone interested in coming to a game?"

"When they aren't even in California and find our secret chatroom, then yes."

"How about this? You can personally vet me. I was planning on bringing a friend. We'll still be in Mexico for several months. Get to know both of us, and if you don't like us, we'll disappear, and when we get to California, we won't go anywhere near a softball game."

"And if I say no?"

"We'll both find out your jersey number and show up to a game wearing nothing but tutus and your jersey number painted on us."

I find myself laughing. I didn't know shit about this guy or his friend, but I have this feeling he would keep his promise. I almost want to tell him no, just to see him do it.

"Fine. But we need our own chatroom. I don't know if you joined to stalk one of the other players, and if I think it's me you're after, I'll have you banned from the game. What's your name?"

"Aeron. My friend is Leif. Call our chatroom Revelations."

"You aren't some weird-ass person trying to save my soul, are you?"

"Not at all. We are just two awesome guys who are fans of softball."

"I have a feeling you are weird."

"You have no idea."

I bolted to a sitting position. Aeron groaned and tried to pull me back into his arms. I poked him in the side like he did to me, and I hated it when he did.

"Revelations! You found our secret chatroom and pretended to be into softball. We made that chatroom so I could make sure you weren't stalkers."

Aeron grinned and stretched on the bed.

"We totally would have shown up to your game in tutus to get your attention."

I started giggling. "You might have met the bad end of Smurfette. It sounds like you've always been looking for me."

"Isaiah has been on our radar for a long time. Way before Armilus started pitching their water supplement. He kept you this big secret. He kept you close, but no one knew he had a daughter. His name is not on your birth certificate, and you never had his last name. All of your schools just thought you were his ward.

"He slipped up. He's a crafty asshole, but there's no firewall Leif and I can't get through. All the data from the clinic you were at as a child was on a cloud server. He sequenced his DNA and one other person. We looked at the DNA and knew right then and there he had a child somewhere.

"This was after you ran away, so it took some time to

find you. We built a dossier with what we could find out about you. We decided the best way to approach you would be that chatroom. We didn't want to bring Isaiah's attention back to you by approaching you right off."

"What's with all of you and Isaiah? You're younger than he is. I know he's evil because he raised me. How did he get on your radar?"

Aeron looked uncomfortable. He was about to side-step the truth again because he either didn't think I could handle it, or he'd already told me this, and telling it to me again could trigger my memories and hurt me.

"You could say Isaiah Nahum is my mortal enemy."

"Then what am I here for? Are you just going to kill us together when we get to the White House?"

Aeron grabbed me and yanked me back down to my chest. He squeezed me so hard, I couldn't breathe.

"Never think that, Ariel. When we found out he had a child, we knew he experimented on you. What we managed to find out was that you got away. Isaiah left you alone for years, but we also knew he was moving pieces for something big. We were trying to find you to protect you from him.

"We approached you in that chatroom because we wanted you to feel safe enough to come to Mexico and hide. Leif and I weren't counting on us all hitting it off. Yeah, I guess you could say we fell for you, even though we hadn't met in person. We told you the truth, and you agreed to come. I was the one that jumped the fucking gun and alerted Isaiah the three of us were coming together. If I hadn't crossed the border to get you, Isaiah would never have known. We would have had time for you to cross to Mexico, where we could've kept you safe from him. It's my fucking fault you don't have your memories, Ariel."

I buried my face in Aeron's neck and squeezed him back.

"Aeron, it's *his* fucking fault. He was the one who did all this, not you."

"You don't understand, Ariel. It's my job to stop him. When we found out about you, it was up to us to keep you safe."

"I don't know what any of that means, and I'm sure you aren't going to tell me, but I'm still alive. My memories are coming back. I might get us banished from California if I don't magically remember how to give a tattoo, but I'm not dead yet. I may kill *you* because I get so pissed off at you that you are keeping secrets from me that don't involve my memories."

"You forget something, Ariel. Most of the things you are asking about, we've had that conversation before. I know exactly what your reaction was the first time I told you. I can't keep you safe if you flip your shit and run."

"Aeron, cannibal corpses are running around, and I slept through World War III. My father did experiments on me, and something in my blood reanimated corpses. I think I'm doing okay with fucked up."

"I know it doesn't seem like it, but things can and will get even more fucked up. I found you just in time."

Aeron might frustrate the piss out of me, not telling me things, but I knew he was doing it to protect me. I hadn't thought about the fact that he already knew how I would react because we'd had this conversation before. Aeron had spent this entire journey trying to make the apocalypse as less shitty for me as he could.

Aeron was doing all these things for me, and sure, I'd

helped having his back looting stores, but I needed to do something for Aeron right now. I fought my way out of his arms and sat on his chest. I pinned his arms by his head, and he just let me. I got right by his face.

"Listen here, Aeron, with no last name. I will break your face if you keep insisting all of this is your fault. I don't remember shit, but there's one thing I do know. *You will always find me.* You will keep me safe no matter what. You *always* have a plan, even if it's crazy and involves your horse murdering corpses. We went the long way, but we did finally meet in person, and I'm remembering. Eventually, I'll remember everything, and you can tell me the truth. Even though I can't remember everything we talked about and you frustrate the shit out of me, I'm glad it was you that found me. I'm glad I'm on the road with you. I'm glad you kissed me that day, and I want more kisses. I enjoy sleeping in your arms. I want—"

Aeron didn't let me finish. He wrestled me onto my back, and now I was the one pinned down. His silver eyes were doing that thing again where I swore they were glowing. He nipped at my nose.

"Speedy wants more kisses?"

Aeron looked flat out dangerous right now, and I didn't care. I liked Aeron like this. I could feel his erection pressing against my stomach, so I started grinding against it.

"I want it all, Aeron. I want you."

The fire went out in his eyes. He rested his forehead on mine.

"This is wrong. You don't remember me."

"Does it count that I like every frustrating inch of you I've managed to get to know since I woke up?"

Aeron let out this frustrated roar and flopped on his back.

"I want to, Speedy. More than you could possibly know. But not until you have your memories back and not until you know the truth about everything. We should find food."

Who knew amnesia was such a cockblocker?

TWENTY-FOUR

I thought Aeron would take it easy now that we weren't surrounded by Rage Heads and humans who had gone feral and were eating people. But no, we were back on the road at a punishing pace, and I just wanted to slow down. Even though a lot of the buildings were still rubble, and they were trying to get the grass to grow again, they had gotten a lot rebuilt. California was a paradise compared to the rest of the world.

I wanted to stay here longer, but really, I just wanted to avoid Sacramento. Aeron was taking us there as fast as he could. We stayed at the hotel rooms Jade had given him. We had hot showers and hot meals every night, and I was grateful for that. It was nice going to bed with a full belly and being able to change my clothes every day. Aeron made one stop to pick up underwear for both of us so I had more than three pairs.

I was sure the street signs in California had been vandalized at one point, but someone took them down and replaced them with wooden signs. After days of riding, my stomach dropped to my feet when I saw the sign that we were entering Sacramento. I gripped his arm. I would have felt better with Smurfette in my grip, but I strapped her to the back of Meremoth because of California rules.

"Do I have to do this?"

"I have faith in you, Speedy."

Aeron brought Meremoth up to a high-rise building with the side blown out. It looked like they were in the process of repairing it. We dismounted and went inside. Someone had wired it so it still had electricity, but we still took the stairs. I hoofed it up thirty flights of stairs to the top floor, and my thighs were screaming at me.

The entire top floor looked like Jade's throne room. They had knocked all the walls down. She was sitting in a La-Z-Boy recliner surrounded by people with guns and satellite phones. She grinned when she saw us, but she didn't stand up.

"Well, well. I've been waiting to meet you since I heard you were here. Why weren't you in California when this all went down?"

"I kind of got a little kidnapped."

Jade cocked an eyebrow at me. Aeron was right. She was tiny. She probably came up to my armpits, and she was dressed in all leather. Her hair was bright red and flowed down her back like a crimson river. She had a considerable septum ring in her nose. I had a feeling I would like her if I didn't fuck up her tattoo, and she killed me.

"And no one ate you? You don't look like some gang ran you ragged using you as bait. Were you eating people, Speedy?"

"I was in a coma. Aeron found me. I'm sorry, but all

my memories are gone. They are coming back in pieces. I don't remember a fucking thing about giving a tattoo. I'll probably end up permanently messing you up."

"Nonsense," Jade said, lighting up a homemade cigarette. "I saw you at a tattoo convention. You were one of the top speakers. I stood in line for hours to get a tattoo from you. The line was out the fucking door, and I missed you. You were always booked a year in advance, and I never knew when I would end up in Los Angeles to book that far out. Now that you're here, I'm getting my tattoo, but my idea has changed."

"Yes, but even with all that backstory, the fact that I can't remember how hasn't changed."

"I know. I have a plan. Do you see this pumpkin at my feet? They are in high demand, and I had one in my vegetable basket this week. I'm forgoing pumpkin pie so you can figure it out on my pumpkin. If you do it, you tattoo me. If the pumpkin is a hot mess, then you'll just have to come back to California and do it when you get your memories back."

At least Jade wasn't totally insane and setting me loose on her body with a tattoo gun. It still didn't solve the problem that I wasn't sure if I could even draw. I hadn't had access to pencils and paper, though sometimes, my hand felt like it should have something in it to sketch with.

One of the gang members presented me with a sketch pad and a pen. It felt like a missing part of me came back when I fitted the pencil in my hand. Maybe I could still draw.

"What do you want me to draw?"

"Okay, I want it on my chest so everyone can see it. I want you to tattoo me on a throne surrounded by zombie heads on pikes. But I want it done Sailor Jerry style."

All of that made sense to some part of my lizard brain. I could already see it in my head and was plotting my lines. I guess I remembered how to draw. I plopped on the floor with my sketch pad in front of Jade.

"Do you want the La-Z-Boy as the throne, or do you want me to improvise?"

"Are you kidding? I want the La-Z-Boy. When this all started out, me and all the girls holed up in a furniture store right near the strip club. We all claimed a recliner and made it our bed. There was a little family-owned grocery store nearby that we could loot. We finally said enough was enough and started taking to the streets to save people when the war started.

"One of the bombs landed in our furniture shop. We weren't there at the time, thank god. But when we visited the rubble, there was my fucking recliner without a scratch on it. This is my lucky recliner, and it deserves to be inked on my chest."

I had a lucky blue baseball bat named Smurfette. She had a lucky recliner. Everyone had the right to be weird right now. I chewed on my bottom lip and focused on my drawing. This just felt right. The scratch of the pen against the paper felt like the first normal thing I'd done since I woke up from that coma, even if I was about to draw a woman dressed like a dominatrix in a recliner surrounded by zombie heads Sailor Jerry style.

This wasn't freaking me out anymore. Jade would not kill me or banish us if I fucked this up. She gave me an out and gave up something she wanted to so I could practice first. She was quite reasonable, which was probably why California was being run so well.

I had a flash of memory. I didn't have a printer with the right paper or anything to transfer this design to her skin when I was done. If they had tracing paper and Speedstick deodorant, it would work in a pinch. I thought that would be way too much to ask for, but Jade managed to produce some.

She had a nice little setup for me to tattoo her on if I could manage the pumpkin. I held up my drawing for her approval.

"Ha! I love it. I really hope you can pull it off on my pumpkin because I'm dying to sport that right across my chest. And I want it as colorful as possible."

I was feeling a little better about this. Holding Smurfette in my hand made it feel like all my missing memories weren't totally horrible, but getting the part of myself back that liked to draw was just a silver lining in the middle of all this shit.

"Can I keep this sketch pad and pen?"

Jade grinned at me. "I got them for you. Things may have gone to shit, but an artist should still be able to create."

"Okay, let me at that pumpkin."

Aeron had been silent this entire time, but when I stood up, he was right there and pulled me into a huge hug. Jade let out a wolf whistle as I stood there pressed against his hard chest.

"You can do this, Speedy. You can do anything you want. You always have."

Aeron had all this faith in me. He handed me my bat like he just knew I could defend myself getting out of that hospital, even though I had no idea who I was. I needed to have more faith in myself.

I didn't make a stencil for the pumpkin. I was just

going to practice. I picked up the tattoo gun. It was heavier than the pencil, but the weight just felt right in my hand. There were little cups for the ink. This was familiar. I used to be able to do this in my sleep. I could do this.

I squirted gel on my paper towel and situated my ink cups in it so they wouldn't fall over. I kicked the gun on and felt the vibrations in my arm. I knew this. I could remember a little. I spent years apprenticing with the best tattoo artist in Los Angeles before I opened my own shop with a great artist I'd met and bonded with at a tattoo convention.

I just knew as I started working on the pumpkin. I knew how much pressure. I knew how deep to go without scarring and I knew how to blend to make just the right color palette. I worked in a haze. I had an image in my head, and I just needed to get it out on the tattoo. I couldn't even say what it was if someone asked me what it was. I would have been pissed if they broke my concentration.

I turned the gun off and stepped back. I didn't even know what I had tattooed on this pumpkin. I looked to see what it was. Aeron peered over my shoulder. I had tattooed four stylized horse heads. One was the color of Meremoth, one was black, one was red, and the other was white. Was this some memory because it didn't make sense?

"What does it mean?" I asked Aeron.

"It means you are getting closer to getting your memories back. And it means you can give Jade something she's been wanting for years. You can spread some light during all this mess."

"That looks like Meremoth and his brothers. If I never

met you before and Meremoth scares the shit out of me, how do I know what his brothers look like?"

"In time, Speedy. Get that tattoo done because I think more of your memories will come back when I get you home."

TWENTY-FIVE

I had so many questions about those four horses I tattooed on the pumpkin, but I knew Aeron would not tell me yet, and I had a job to do. Maybe it would all make sense when we got to Los Angeles. I didn't want to think about why I was drawing strange things on pumpkins. I didn't want to think about bombed-out landscapes or corpses that chased you.

I wanted to feel normal for a few hours, so I threw myself into doing Jade's tattoo. It just felt right, like I was supposed to be doing this. It took several hours, but I eventually finished it. Jade was ecstatic and walked around the entire top floor in just her leather bra to show it off. That was the kind of happy customer I liked.

Jade wouldn't let us leave until she threw a tattoo celebration. It was a strange party, but there was alcohol. Most of it was moonshine and hooch, and I was pretty sure I would end up with hair on my chest after drinking it. They'd made this endless supply of dips from local produce and dairy.

By the time we got back to the hotel room, I had

passed out. Aeron was nowhere near as drunk as the Wild Turkey incident and had to hold my hair back while I puked. How mortifying. He was very gentle when he helped me to bed.

I was hungover as all fuck the next morning, but Aeron wasn't going easy on me. He woke me up at the ass crack of dawn, and I was on the back of Meremoth after breakfast. If I thought riding that horse sober was scary, trying to hang onto that saddle with a raging headache, while I felt like barfing, was much worse.

Aeron kept a punishing pace to Los Angeles. We stopped to sleep only when curfew started, and we would have gotten arrested for being on the street. We were back on the road as soon as curfew allowed us to be back on the street.

I was so tired, but at least I was clean, and my belly was full. I could deal with that because I think we were both banking on a lot of my memories returning at my apartment. Jade's gift was also paying off. That sketch pad was coming in handy, and we'd eventually have to find another.

Before bed, I would sit with my sketch pad and sort of go into this trance. Some things I drew made little sense at all like the four horses. Most of the pictures Aeron would explain to me. The first photo I drew was my father, as I last saw him. Aeron confirmed that for me. I drew him in a trance with devil horns and 666 written across his forehead.

I drew more scenes like the Alice in Wonderland tattoos on my arms. Aeron explained they were my favorite books as a child. My father never gave me any or read to me. It was the only book appropriate for children in his library. I stole them and read them cover to cover all the time. I took his first edition copies when I ran away. Aeron swore they were still at my apartment where I'd left them. He also promised there were still sketchpads all over the place, and he'd make room in his saddlebags so I could take as many as he could carry and us still eat.

I was antsy, and the closer we got to Los Angeles, the more my anxiety grew. What if we got to my apartment, and I didn't remember a fucking thing? What if it seemed like a stranger's home? I knew that would break me. Aeron put all his stock and planned his route to Mexico with a stop there. He had all his hopes in that apartment triggering some of my memories.

It was contagious. I had been gung-ho to get there and start remembering too. But memory loss was tricky. Aeron couldn't even tell me anything because of how it was done to me. My dreams were sporadic. I didn't have them every night. Sometimes, they were pleasant and didn't help me with this puzzle involving my father. Sometimes they were horrible nightmares about the experiments that were done on me when I was a child. I hated those dreams. Whatever they were trying to do, they needed me totally terrorized to do it.

I thought I would have a panic attack when I saw the sign we were entering Los Angeles. Aeron tightened his arm around my waist and nuzzled my neck. He seemed to know exactly what was going on with my lizard brain.

"It's just an apartment, Speedy. Even if you don't remember a thing, you can grab new clothes and some sketchpads. You can look around and see what kind of person you used to be, even if you don't remember a thing. You've faced countless Rage Heads. Don't be afraid of your old home."

"I'm scared I will get there and it will not trigger anything. Or, what if triggers too much and I go crazy?"

"Do you trust me, Speedy?"

"Even though you won't tell me your last name, I do."

Aeron kissed the top of my head.

"I really don't have a last name. Would you prefer I lie and make one up? If you don't remember anything, ask questions, and I'll try to answer what I can. If it's getting to be too much, I'll throw you over my shoulder and get you out of there."

I saw a building up ahead. I knew that building. I was friendly with the doorman. He buzzed me in every day, and he was great about keeping roller derby and softball stalkers out of my building.

"That's my building," I said, pointing.

It looked like it survived the bomb blasts, but I think it must have been in better shape when I lived here before. Dirt covered all the windows, and the paint had faded and was flaking off. I couldn't remember their names, but I think I had been on friendly terms with all of my neighbors.

"What happened to the other people that lived here?"

"Some of them turned into Rage Heads and were eventually killed when California came together. Your neighbor Miss Mabel is still next door. She has to be ninety, and she beat me with a broom when she saw me going into your apartment. Every time I come back through here and check on your place, she threatens me with it. Did you know brooms hurt when you get whacked on the head with one?"

I saw a flash. My next-door neighbor was like a surrogate mother to me. I picked up her cigarettes and Mountain Dew and visited with her after every softball game. She always had homemade cookies waiting and wanted to know all about my game. She'd also told me she knew people who could take care of the softball stalkers. From what I could remember about her, it would take more than some cannibal corpses and bombs to kill Miss Mabel. I was glad she was still here.

"What happened to Derrick, the doorman?"

"Well, I threatened the shit out of him to allow me inside when I realized you were missing, then I made him wet his pants, trying to question him who trashed your place. They did it without getting the broom treatment from Miss Mabel because I questioned her, too, when she stopped hitting me."

"Is he still there?"

"He's not. From what I understand, he died protecting the residents from a horde of Rage Heads before the gangs took to the streets and started fighting. Jade united all the gangs in California, and they've recruited. The new doorman is one of hers."

"Is he going to give me shit?"

"Probably. Don't give it back, or he won't let you inside."

Aeron stopped in front of the building, and we both dismounted. Meremoth did that running off thing. We were in a more urban part of the city, and I couldn't imagine where a huge fucking horse would sleep for the night, but Aeron seemed to think it wasn't a problem, and he already admitted he wasn't a normal horse.

Aeron was right. The man at the door wasn't someone I knew. I barely remembered Derrick, but I was sad he went out like that. I remembered us being friends. The man at the door must have been new because he didn't recognize Aeron either. He barred our way carrying a substantial fucking machete.

"Residents only."

"Her apartment is 5C."

"Bullshit. I've been watching this building for five months, and I've never seen either of you."

Aeron reached into one of his bags and pulled out his keyring. There was one of those fancy keys with a fox on it. The man at the door narrowed his eyes at it.

"Where have you been for the last five months, then?"

"Ariel?" I heard someone shriek. "Girl, get your ass over here and give an old woman a hug. I thought you were dead. George, push off. She lived here before all this, and I've been looking after her apartment. Aeron secured it after someone broke in. Let them in."

"You know these people, Miss Mabel?"

"Yeah, I do. Let them in."

The man lowered his machete and let us through. Miss Mabel wrapped her arm around my waist and led me inside.

"You don't know how good it is to see you, girl. You haven't kept up the pink in your hair. Did you want me to do it? You always said I was the only one you trusted to do your hair. I might still have some pink left."

I knew there might be answers in my old apartment, but my gut was telling me I needed to sit and visit with Miss Mabel. She needed it just as much as I did. From what I could remember, we had been close. I did her grocery shopping, and she did my hair.

"Let's just sit and chat. We need to catch up."

Miss Mabel pat my arm.

"If I had known you would show up out of the blue today randomly, I would have had your favorite cookies waiting. Luckily yours don't involve chocolate because they don't give that out in your weekly basket. The only way to get chocolate now is to trade sex for it. I wouldn't mind getting laid, but I'd have to question some of these children who will trade chocolate for sex with a granny."

"I can get you chocolate with no strings, Miss Mabel," Aeron said.

She just let out a little grunt.

"You might be built like a stallion and brought my Speedy home safely, but you aren't getting chocolate here without dicking someone."

I was trying so hard not to laugh. I ended up snorting, and then I laughed at the snort. I could see why I was friends with this woman. She was sassy, and she could even put Aeron in his place. He was the color of an eggplant, and he was usually unflappable.

"How about you both come over for dinner? I've got fresh bread cooling, and I got some lovely vegetables with my eggs in my box this week. I made a quiche."

"We don't want to eat all your food."

"Nonsense. I might not be able to get chocolate, but I get plenty of food. The world might be ending, and people have gone feral, but we don't stand for that in California. A lot of the people who lived in this building before you went missing are dead. Aeron here got them to agree to keep your apartment as it was, and I've been tending to it. Most of the people who got assigned the empty apartments here were people that got injured in the war.

"This building didn't take a lot of damage, and there's that medical clinic on the corner. They send me extra food because they know I host potlucks for the entire building sometimes. It's not the same people, but this building is just as close as it used to be."

Miss Mabel had a ground-floor apartment. I was glad she didn't have to deal with that staircase we passed. As soon as I stepped inside, I had a massive flood of memories. Her apartment was homey and full of knickknacks. I remembered this place. I spent a lot of time here.

I moved in here as a fifteen-year-old runaway with stolen money for my deposit and no job. Miss Mabel caught me in the hall with my one backpack struggling to unlock the door and saw right through me and just adopted me right there on the spot. I think I spilled more of my secrets to her than I ever did to any of my girls on the softball team.

I couldn't help it. I was so glad she was still alive. I flung my arms around her neck and gave her a huge hug. I didn't see my mother in any of my memories, and I just got this feeling she wasn't around when I was growing up. Miss Mabel filled that role for me, and that was why I'd never moved out of this apartment.

"Damn, Speedy. Not so hard. I missed you too."

I wiped the tears from my eyes.

"Miss Mabel, so many of my memories are gone, but I remember the first day we met. I remember how close we were. I was so nervous about coming back here and not remembering anything. I'm so glad you're still here."

She pat my back.

"It will take more than walking corpses and World War III to kill Mabel Eastman. I found this sexy drink of water going through your things the day you told me you would be going away for a little while. I gave him what for with my broom until he told me you were supposed to meet him and went missing. I helped him go through your apartment and clean it up. Your laptop was missing, and so was your cell phone. We both think you would have taken those with you when you left, so they would have had those when they grabbed you. We still don't know what they were after."

I shrugged.

"I don't either. I don't even remember what my apartment looks like."

"Let's not talk about that right now. Let's celebrate Aeron found you and brought you home safe."

Miss Mabel's entire apartment smelled like fresh-baked bread, and her quiche looked delicious. We started serving ourselves, but I'd have to break the news to her we weren't staying—this kind of changed things. I found a home in California when I ran. Miss Mabel was my family, and she was still here.

I could stay here. California seemed relatively safe, considering what was going on with the rest of the world. Miss Mabel helped me find my first job and enroll in college. She brought me to set up my first bank account and taught me how to balance a checkbook. She had been there for me when I was totally lost.

I had this feeling when I agreed to go to Mexico with Aeron and Leif, I had every intention of coming back. Miss Mabel had to be in her nineties now. She made it through the apocalypse and was still taking care of people. It was my turn to take care of her.

"Aeron, I—"

"Let me stop you right there, Ariel," Miss Mabel said. "I know what the next words out of your mouth will be. You never could hide anything from me. You told me you were going to Mexico because your father was planning something big and you had to stop him. I know all about what that evil man did to you. The day after you went missing, the shit started hitting the fan. You had a plan with Aeron to stop him before you went missing. Now that he's found you, you can't rest yet.

"The Ariel I know wouldn't give up and hide in California over an old lady. She would fight to get her memories back and beat her father."

"What if I do beat him? What if I come back to California and you aren't here? Someone needs to be taking care of you."

"I say this with all kindness. Shut the fuck up, Ariel. The day I turn into a helpless old lady who needs a nursemaid, I want a bullet to the head. If I die while you're off taking care of your father, I'll be an angel on your shoulder looking out for you."

I took in a breath and tried not to let the tears fall. I still couldn't remember my apartment, but I remembered everything about Miss Mabel. She married her high school sweetheart, and he died in a tragic accident before their first anniversary. They didn't have any children, and she never remarried. It didn't seem fair that I wouldn't get to stay here with her to make her life more comfortable.

"But—"

"No buts, Ariel. I made Aeron tell me everything. I know his friend can end some of this with your blood. That is way more important than hanging out in my apartment with me. I don't like them as much as I like you, but I have friends and people who check in on me here."

"It's just not fair."

"Young lady, you got kidnapped, your memories are going, it's the end of the world, and *that* is what you think is unfair? None of this is fair. We do what we have to. Get your shit together and stop the apocalypse."

"You're right. You'd better be here when I get back. I'll be furious at you if you aren't."

"That's my girl. Now I know your apartment better than Aeron does. Now that we are done eating, let's go see if we can get some of your memories back."

Well, here goes nothing.

Twenty-Six

My apartment was right next door. Miss Mabel and Aeron both had a key. Aeron was fiddling with the lock. I remembered that first day I tried to unlock the door. Miss Mabel stopped me in the hall and told me I had to jiggle it because the lock stuck. I guess no one decided the apocalypse warranted a lock change.

I stepped into my apartment with my eyes closed. Who was I before this aside from a tattoo artist who played softball with an evil father? Did I decorate the place in some sort of gaudy décor? Did I have music in this apartment that would embarrass new me? Aeron held one hand, and Miss Mabel held the other.

"Open your eyes, Ariel," Aeron said.

I cracked my eyes open. I had painted my walls a smokey gray, and it looked like I had gone for some vintage vibe with my furniture. I covered every surface in art. There were paintings and sculptures all over the place. The only wall that wasn't covered in pictures had a wall to wall bookcase that was full of books.

I was getting little flashes. This place was a total shit-hole when I moved in. There was a dingy floral wallpaper and shag carpet that was leftover from the seventies. Miss Mabel made some phone calls and got me hooked up with a few people in the art scene. When my art started selling, I had the carpet pulled up and hardwood put in. I ripped the wallpaper down and repainted. All my furniture was carefully from thrift stores.

"Have my walls always been that color?"

Miss Mable just laughed.

"Sweetie, you painted the walls a different color when-ever your mood changed, and sometimes, you could be a real moody bitch. You went through your blue period on these walls."

"Is all this art mine?"

"The art on your walls changed too. You hung it in the living room until it was time to take it to the gallery to be sold. If I said I liked one, you always wanted to give it to me. I have several of your paintings in my apartment. The ones you liked too much to sell are in your bedroom."

I studied the paintings harder. They were themed. It was those fucking horses again. They were painted differ-ently than what I tattooed on the pumpkins, but they still looked like fierce war horses. They were the same colors I chose for the pumpkin, and one looked suspiciously like Meremoth.

I narrowed my eyes at Aeron.

"Why was I working on those horses, and why was the first thing I tattooed on those pumpkins when I went in a trance four horses? You said Meremoth wasn't a normal horse, and there were only four like him. One of those horses looks *exactly* like your horse."

"Ariel, you always painted what was going on in your life unless it was a commissioned tattoo."

Miss Mabel smacked Aeron on the back of the head. She hit him pretty hard too. God, I loved that woman.

"If you won't tell her, I will."

"You will scare her."

"Oh, shut up. I've known this girl longer than you have. She doesn't scare easily. If she hasn't figured it out yet, she has a right to know. It could probably help your happy ass right now."

"Someone better tell me, or I have a feeling I can throw a pretty epic temper tantrum."

Aeron ran his fingers through his hair and started pacing.

"You know how long I looked for her, right? When I finally found her, she didn't even remember her own name, much less me. I can't just tell her everything without hurting her. I've been spending this entire journey here trying to ease her into everything and gaining her trust. You could ruin everything, Mabel."

I blocked Aeron's path. I crossed my arms and tried to stare him down.

"If you want me to trust you, then you will let her tell me why I keep painting those horses. If you want to keep making a stink about it, you can turn around, walk out that door, and go to Mexico without me."

"Ariel—"

"No, Aeron! Every time I've had a memory, you've explained things to me and given me more of my past. I haven't been hurt. Those horses came from somewhere when I tattooed that pumpkin, and now, they are all over my apartment. I want to know what it means!"

Aeron grumbled and plopped on my couch. This

huge, horse riding, sword-wielding man was pouting like a child.

"I would tell you when you had more of your memories back," he muttered.

"You said you tattooed these horses on a pumpkin? What in hell were you doing tattooing pumpkins, Ariel?" Miss Mabel demanded.

"Well, Jade wanted a tattoo from me, but I didn't remember how. She sacrificed one pumpkin from her basket for me to practice on."

"Let me guess. Your vision blurred, and you had no idea what you were drawing until you finished."

"Yes, exactly. I had no idea I had drawn those four horses until I finished."

"That's how you created all your art, Ariel. Until you learned to disguise it better, so it wasn't as obvious, a lot of things in your paintings eventually came true. It's why you ran away from your father. After he stopped bringing you to that lab, there was a room he would lock you in. It was a padded room with a drawing desk. He'd lock you in there after school and terrorize you until you drew something like it was some sort of exact science. You made him a rich man until you ran away."

Why didn't I see any of that shit when I was getting flashes? And how exactly was I drawing the future in these trances? How did something in my blood cause the Rage mutation? I really needed a fucking drink.

"If Meremoth is not a normal horse, then I guess I'm not a normal girl either, am I?"

Miss Mabel clapped her hands.

"We need supplies. Aeron, go back to my apartment and get the cigar box on top of the fridge. I know exactly how to handle this."

I was glad someone did because I sure as hell didn't. I could remember that I talked to Miss Mabel about everything. Fuck, we even talked about my sex life. I trusted her enough to tell her about the visions in the past.

"Did we talk when I painted these horses? Did we ever figure out what it meant?"

"You painted those right around the time you met Aeron and Leif in that chatroom. You kept asking if I thought they were creeps, and you should ban them from the softball game. Then, you got to know them. You became obsessed with the Book of Revelations trying to figure out why you kept painting different versions of those four horses. Those four horses are from the bible."

"But from what I can remember, I wasn't religious at all."

"No, child, you weren't. You took the Lord's name in vain all the time, and the fucking church would have exploded if you set foot inside without getting doused in Holy Water first. But those visions of yours came from somewhere, and I don't think it was from down below."

"So, the horses are important. I don't remember a fucking thing about the Book of Revelations."

"No, but I do. I watched it play out. That right there is the Black Horse. His rider brings pestilence and famine. We saw that with the Rage mutation. One rider down. The Red Horse is said to bring war. We already had that. World War III wiped several countries off the map. The White Horse is supposed to bring conquest. After governments started falling during the wars, people were swooping in and seizing power. Entire countries were getting absorbed into other countries and renamed. The Pale Horse brings death.

"Rage Heads outnumber humans and food is scarce

unless you happen to live somewhere people decided to work together instead of fight. There are other states like California, where they have rebuilt homes, are breeding livestock, and planting. They've walled up the entire state to keep the Rage Heads out, and their rules may even be stricter than Jade's. It's not everywhere because some people don't want a community, they want to rule the roost, but they are out there."

Aeron had a pale horse that wasn't a normal horse. He said several times his specialty was death. Could I trust Aeron? How did I know he was trying to get me to Mexico so his friend could figure out why the AB negative people didn't turn with the rest of the population when they poisoned the water?

Suddenly, my traveling companion, who I was pretty sure I was starting to have feelings for, was starting to seem pretty dangerous. I knew him before in that chatroom, and I agreed to go to Mexico with him for some reason, but he was in that chatroom just to get to me. He sought me out and planned for us to go to our private room, eventually.

Fuck, had he been playing me this entire time? Was the real reason he didn't want to tell me anything was because I had figured something out and had tried to get away from him? Did Aeron put me in that fucking coma, and the only reason he came back was that the place had been overrun with Rage Heads?

Shit, he was right next door, and he was coming back. If he was really dangerous, and I ran, he might hurt Miss Mabel. Where could I go, anyway? Aeron had connections all over California, and I was pretty sure everyone I knew except Miss Mabel was dead. I could go to Jade, but Aeron would get there first since he had Meremoth. She also knew him better than she knew me and had more reason to trust him.

"I don't think we can trust Aeron," I whispered.

"What makes you say that?"

I pointed to the Pale Horse I'd painted surrounded by death.

"Because I've ridden on that horse. It belongs to Aeron, and he's already admitted it's not a normal horse."

Miss Mabel pat my hand.

"I know you've had shitty luck with men, my dear, but you didn't see him the day you went missing. He was distraught and blaming himself. He couldn't fake that."

"What if I drew something and saw he was dangerous? What if he staged the entire thing because he found out I would run?"

"He's here. You're here. You've got a broom I can beat him with, and you've been clutching Smurfette like you think someone will steal her from you. Just question him. Or, grab a sketch pad and see if anything comes to you."

"What did you send him for?"

Miss Mabel just grinned at me.

"You looked like you needed to relax. Most of the booze now is hard to find and homemade. It tastes like something you'd use to run your car with. The marijuana growers got things up and running as soon as they got the power grid back up."

"Aw, and you will share your pot stash with us? What's the occasion? You made me bring my own when we smoked up together before."

Miss Mabel pinched my arm.

"Don't say I did nothing nice to you. Maybe if we get Aeron high, he'll get that stick out of his ass."

Have I mentioned how much I love this woman?

TWENTY-SEVEN

Aeron came back with a vintage cigar box and a confused look on his face. Miss Mabel and I were huddled together on my sofa, trying to figure that motherfucker out. She thought I should trust him and go with him to Mexico, but I had my doubts. I put my life in Aeron's hands, and I believed him when he told me he couldn't give me my life back right away, but why didn't he want me to know about those paintings or that I could draw things like that? *Why* could I draw stuff like that?

"Is getting high really the best use of our time?" Aeron said. "I would let Ariel explore her apartment to see if it triggered her memories, then we need to get back on the road."

"Why didn't you want me to know about those photos, Aeron? Why didn't you want Miss Mabel to tell me about what happens when I paint?"

Aeron flopped on my armchair and started expertly rolling joints with Miss Mabel's stash.

"So, I guess we are doing this, or you won't leave with

me? After everything we went through on the road, you don't trust me."

"That's Meremoth on my wall, Aeron. I keep painting four horses. There are four horses in the Book of Revelations that bring about the end of the world. My train of thought is that I saw all this when I was painting, realized you were involved and painted you this way. I tried to get away at the diner, and it was you and your team that stuck me in that coma and took my memories."

Aeron looked like I just ran over his puppy on purpose, then backed up and ran over it a second time. Miss Mabel just lit up her joint and took a huge hit.

"Can you blame her, Aeron? After her father, she doesn't really have any reason to trust men, and you made a scene about the paintings."

"Fuck it. I will need to get high to have this conversation."

Miss Mabel was leaning back on my sofa with her eyes in slits.

"That's Purple Panther. It's guaranteed to get that stick out your ass."

There was a lot I couldn't remember, but I could remember everything about Miss Mabel. She'd never tell me her source, but she could always find the best weed, and she pretty much never shared with me. After she told me it helped with her arthritis, I stopped asking and brought my own when we smoked together. She must have been in a sharing mood if she was breaking out her stash for two more people.

Aeron took a long inhale and glared at me.

"If I was trying to hurt you, why would I bring you back here? I came back here after you went missing. I knew these paintings were on the wall, and I knew Mabel was still here. I was hoping she was still around when I managed to get you here. If I were trying to hide something from you, I would have killed her and destroyed these paintings if bringing you back here was this huge ruse."

Well, fuck. He had some damned good points. And Miss Mabel liked him, or she wouldn't be sharing her weed with him. She could sniff out an evil person like one of those truffle pigs. I remembered a guy I dated that I was totally into, and she hated. She kept telling me to dump him, and I didn't listen. I found out epically and the hard way that when Miss Mabel said someone's mother should have just swallowed, you should stay away from that person. And she wasn't doing that with Aeron.

"Then why didn't you want me to know I paint the future?"

"Ariel, you only woke up a few weeks ago. You found out corpses are eating people, humanity has gone to shit, they have bombed most of the world, and you are dealing with horrible nightmares of what your father did to you. I would tell you when you'd had time to come to terms with that. I was hoping to tell you when you stopped waking up screaming."

Fair enough, but Aeron needed to stop deciding for me what I could and couldn't handle. He'd passed part of my test, but there was still an enormous question that he would need to answer if I would go to Mexico with him or stay here with Miss Mabel.

"Why did I paint your horse as something out of the Book of Revelations, Aeron?"

I didn't really believe the Book of Revelations was happening. I knew Miss Mabel's theory. It made sense, but there was this part of me that just thought men wrote the bible to control people. It was a fairy tale. But something made me paint those horses and start reading it, and it was probably the shit happening now.

Aeron had that look on his face. I knew it quite well by now. He didn't want to tell me, and he knew I would not take it well. I wasn't near high enough to deal with another lie. If he didn't answer my question, I was booting him out of my apartment and riding out the apocalypse with Miss Mabel.

"The answer is in your bedroom, Ariel," Aeron said.

"Oh, that's right!" Miss Mabel said. "I forgot about that one. I showed it to you when I stopped beating you with the broom and realized who you were."

"You're dangerous with a broom, Mabel. When you want to keep a painting from a series, you hang it in your bedroom. You kept one from these horse paintings, and you hung it right above your bed because it meant a lot to you."

"You'd best take a toke off that joint before you go in there, Speedy," Miss Mabel said.

If Miss Mabel thought I needed to be good and high to view some vision painting I decided to keep that would answer whether or not I should go to Mexico with Aeron, I'd smoke this entire joint because I already wasn't high enough to hear that I could paint the future.

Aeron was jiggling his knee and looked like he wanted me to hurry the fuck up and go in my bedroom. Honestly, he was ruining what little high I had. I just wanted five minutes to process all this shit. What was I, anyway? Some sort of psychic? I wasn't sure I believed in all that. No one could see the future.

Still, there was a lot of shit staring me in the face that I couldn't deny. I was drawing those horses back then and now for a reason. Aeron was somehow right in the middle of it. I didn't *want* Aeron to be the bad guy. I didn't want the reason that I kept drawing these horses because Aeron had been working for my father this entire time. I didn't want to know I had bought his lies this whole time.

There was apparently some sort of proof in my bedroom, but I was stalling going in there. Because I might not remember a lot of things and I might not know if I could trust Aeron, but there was one thing I knew. Miss Mabel would never lie to me. If she were beating the shit out of Aeron with a broom, she only would have stopped for a principled reason. If he came at her, she would have snapped it in half and drove part of that broom through his neck.

I was pretty fucking high, but still not high enough to deal with my bedroom. This was the apocalypse. I was lucky even to have weed to deal with this shit. I also didn't have the luxury of trying to get my shit together before I went in there.

I stood up and glared at Aeron.

"I'm going in there alone. You wait here."

I hadn't seen a single Rage Head behind the walls of California, and I already knew that doorman wouldn't allow strangers in, but I grabbed Smurfette like she could protect me from whatever the fuck I had painted before I got kidnapped.

I flipped the light on and stepped inside. I didn't need to find this mysterious painting among all the pictures hung on my bedroom wall. It was huge, and I'd hung it right above my bed. I stared at that thing, and I could only do one thing.

"What the fuck is this shit?" I shrieked.

Miss Mabel came ambling in and stood next to me and stared at it.

"It's a lot kinkier than what you usually show me, but this is what made up your mind to meet Aeron and Leif."

Aeron peered around the corner of the door.

"Is anyone feeling like they will hit me with something if I come in?"

"The jury is still out."

The painting above my bed was hyper realistic and less stylized than the horses. It was also horrifyingly erotic. It was me standing in the middle of the Oval Office. Aeron was there with three other men. The Oval Office was totally trashed, and my shirt was half off. I was kissing one man on the mouth while the other men were kissing various parts of me. It looked like we were all about to fuck in the middle of a destroyed Oval Office.

"*This* is supposed to convince me? I painted some wet dream, and that is supposed to answer all my questions?"

"Ariel, do you promise not to beat me with Smurfette if I come in your bedroom?"

"Explain from the door, and I'll decide."

"Your father wasn't president when you painted that. The men in that painting are my team, and we weren't fully formed yet. The man kissing you is Dice, and the man kissing your shoulder is Asher. You knew Leif and I. You had photos of us, but you didn't know Dice and Asher because they hadn't joined us yet.

"We knew your father was planning something big, but we didn't know what. *You* were the one that told us his plans eventually involved inserting himself as president. When you saw that, you called Leif and me on three-way and said you would come to help us stop him."

"It's true, Ariel. You came barging into my apartment

right in the middle of *The Bachelorette*, and you knew not to bother me during my show. You were ranting about how your father would become president and how you had to go to Mexico so you could stop him. We talked every night about your chat friends. You were trying to figure out if you could trust them or if they were really working for your father. When you painted yourself with them like this, you knew you could. Your visions *always* come true, Ariel."

I pointed Smurfette at Aeron, who was still hiding behind the door frame.

"I'm *not* having an orgy with you and your friends in the Oval Office."

Aeron held up his hands in surrender.

"No one is forcing you. Are we past this nonsense that I'm working for your father now?"

"That depends. Are you past your nonsense where you keep secrets from me, and you decide when you think I'm ready to hear something?"

Aeron sighed.

"Fine! But if I tell you something and you flip your shit, keep your bat to yourself."

"Are you going to explain the horses now?"

"This is very biblical, Ariel. Pestilence, War, Conquest, and Death. We've had all of those. You saw that and painted it. Your paintings weren't always as realistic as what's above your bed. Some were just symbolism, and you didn't know what it meant until something happened."

"He's right, Ariel. Sometimes, we'd sit and try to figure out what your paintings meant, and it never made sense until something hit the news."

"But that's *your* horse, Aeron!"

"Sit down, Ariel," Miss Mabel said. "You're focusing on one small thing instead of the big picture. The horse is just a symbol. You need to be worrying about why you saw something out of the Book of Revelations when you painted this series, and it's all come to pass. I know more about the bible than you do. You always thought it was a fairy tale. If this is biblical, it only gets worse from here. All of this is just the start."

"She's right, Ariel. It's about to get much worse, and we need you. You saw this, and you painted it. This ends in the Oval Office."

"With an orgy, apparently. I don't even know you assholes."

Aeron just smirked at me.

"Dice and Asher don't know you either. They might have opinions about this painting too. Leif liked you in chat, but he might change his mind if you threaten him with Smurfette like you do me. We might not want to have an orgy with you either."

Well, that was just offensive.

"So, I guess we are going to Mexico, then going to D.C. to kill the President where we *will not* be having an orgy in the Oval Office later."

Aeron visibly relaxed.

"We can't stay here long, Ariel. Catch up with Mabel and try to remember as much as you can, but then we have to leave."

What I wouldn't give to just hang out with Miss Mabel and pretend like none of this was going on. But apparently, I could draw the future, and my father managed to put something biblical in motion. I had no idea how the fuck we were supposed to stop that, but killing him would undoubtedly make me feel better.

TWENTY-EIGHT

I spent a lot of time in my bedroom studying the paintings I chose to keep. I was hoping it would give me some sort of clue to the things I painted before I went missing. Some of them had symbols I couldn't even begin to guess what they were, and some were so abstract, I was letting my eyes blur and looking for a sailboat. They weren't nearly as apparent as the painting I hung above my bed. What the fuck was I doing that I even painted that?

Miss Mabel and Aeron were in my room, trying to help me put together the mystery of my art. Miss Mabel was here when I painted them and chose to keep them. Aeron had only been in my apartment a few times as far as I knew, but he seemed to know what all of those strange symbols meant, and I didn't take him for being into art or different languages.

Aeron spoke freely about all the paintings in my bedroom, but he was tightlipped about the horses. One of these paintings was about the bombing of a sacred site in Iraq. I painted a tsunami that killed thousands of people.

One was a hate crime in Georgia. They were all these huge disasters where people got killed. I don't know how Aeron figured that out because it wasn't totally obvious looking at the painting.

Did I ever paint anything nice like puppies and kittens? What about a lovely still life? Were all my visions doom and gloom?

"Should I try again? I mean, if I painted he would end up in the Oval Office, and it happened, should I try to figure out what's next?"

"We know what's next, Ariel. We have to take him off the playing field before it happens."

"Are you letting me in on this, or is it a big secret?"

"The Book of Revelations is his playbook. It's written that there are three and a half years of peace before the next wave of shit hits the fan. World War III ended three years ago. We only have half a year to stop him before things get even worse. I found you just in time."

Miss Mabel gave Aeron some epic stink eye.

"I know what the painting in her bedroom says, and her paintings always come true, but if you put her in danger, I'll do worse to you than beat you with my broom. And no Oval Office orgies! Don't get fresh with her! Ariel, beat him with Smurfette if he tries anything."

Yeah, the colossal problem was, until I saw those horses on my wall, I *wanted* him to get fresh with me. He was still hot as hell, and I couldn't deny that I always felt safe with him. Now, I was confused, and I hated feeling like this.

I remembered enough about my bedroom that I kept my sketchpads underneath the drafting table in the corner. I had no idea how to trigger one of these visions, but I had to try. I stalked over to my drafting table and whipped out a sketchpad. I pulled my box out and found a piece of charcoal.

My vision blurred, and my hand just started moving. I couldn't tell what was going on in the surrounding room. I was only focused on getting something down on this piece of paper. I could hear the scratch of the charcoal against the paper, but all I could see was a blur. I couldn't stop. I couldn't stop drawing until I finished it.

Finally, my hand stilled. It was over. I blinked until my vision went back into focus. I had no idea what I had just drawn. I looked down and realized that if I really could draw the future, we were totally fucked.

I had drawn an angel with a fiery sword slaying a demon. I guess all that blustering about the Book of Revelations being a fairytale was me talking out my ass. If this really would happen, then we didn't have a lot of time to get to Washington and kill my father. How was my father even doing all this?

Aeron and Miss Mabel peered over my shoulder.

"I think we'd better leave for Mexico in the morning if this drawing will come true."

TWENTY-NINE

As much as I wanted to stay in Los Angeles with Miss Mabel, it wasn't possible. My father was bringing the Book of Revelations to life, and I was apparently some mutant who could draw the future and whose blood could mutate people into cannibal corpses. If we managed to end this, that shit wouldn't look good on a resume at all.

I wept like a total child as I hugged Miss Mabel goodbye the next morning. I made her swear to be there still when I got back. And I intended to come back. My father fucked up my life for too long. I would not stand for this. I'd bash his brains in with Smurfette.

Aeron let me say goodbye for as long as I wanted before Miss Mabel finally shooed me away and told me I had a job to do. She also made me swear I'd come back. It was later than usual, but we were back on the road. I'd stopped asking Aeron where Meremoth went in California or how he managed to eat when we were staying in hotels or my apartment. I was dying to know, but I knew he wouldn't tell me. It was probably something fucking biblical.

We made our way through California, stopping at hotels for the night. I would miss the comforts California offered. We had proper beds and hot food every night. And apparently, you could get good weed if you had the hookup like Miss Mabel.

By the time we got to the gate to leave, something was wrong. There was a massive crowd at the entrance and men with guns at the top. Personally, I thought we should go the other way, but Aeron rode straight up to them.

"What's going on?"

"The Skull Brotherhood is trying to break in. It looks like they've joined up with three other gangs we've refused to let in. They are heavily armed. We are waiting for reinforcements, but they cut a tree down, and they are using it to batter down the gate."

Just then, the entire wall shook, and gunshots rang out. Aeron snapped to attention.

"Why isn't there more shooting?"

The man at the gate looked furious. He ran his hand over his bald scalp and glared at Aeron.

"Yeah, we already thought of that, dickhead. They built some sort of shield wall out of car doors like they think they are fucking Vikings."

Aeron hopped off Meremoth. Before I could dismount, he smacked the horse on the ass.

"You know what to do, boy."

That fucking horse bolted away from the gate with his super-speed, leaving Aeron behind and me wondering what the fuck was going on. Didn't they need as many people as possible at the gate fighting? Was Aeron fucking benching me? He had no problem fighting Rage Heads with me, but we couldn't fight humans trying to destroy what California had built?

I was so fucking pissed off, and there was no way I could jump off Meremoth running this fast without getting hurt. I didn't think the horse would ever stop running. And when he did, I had no idea why he stopped at the door of a bar. Meremoth stopped right at the front door and only gave me enough room to dismount and go inside.

I managed to get myself off the back of Meremoth ungracefully and tried to find the gate again to join the fight. Meremoth blocked whatever path I tried to take that wasn't inside the bar. Can I say I hated it when Aeron and his fucking horse collaborated against me?

"Fine!" I yelled, throwing up my hands. "You're both a horse's ass."

I stomped into the bar, and it was totally empty except one lone bartender. I plopped at the bar and pouted.

"Did you get benched by a fucking horse too?"

"Excuse me?"

"There's a fight at the gate. I'd rather be there helping."

"So would I, but I lost my leg in the war. Why'd they send you away?"

"I'm traveling with a man who thinks he always knows what's best for me."

"Fuck him, right? Well, you're here. What will you have?"

"What are my options?"

"I've got a small brewery in the back. I can't brew a lot because the supplies just aren't there, but I can either get you a beer or a whiskey. It's all rationed. You can only have two bottles of beer or three shots of whiskey, so choose wisely. House rules. I couldn't stay in business if I let everyone get sloppy drunk every night."

"I don't have any money."

"Where the fuck have you been? Money is worthless now. It's all about barter now."

"All I have are clothes that you'd look stupid in, my bat, and a sketch pad."

If I didn't believe I could draw the future when I first heard it, this guy definitely would not give me a beer if I tried to tell him that. He'd probably boot my ass out his bar for fibbing.

"Tell you what. I'll cut you a break since you'd be at that wall fighting if you could. Draw me a pretty picture for my bar, and I'll give you a beer."

"What would you like me to draw?"

"Surprise me."

Oh, how I would have preferred him telling me what to draw. Apparently, when you set me loose with a sketchpad, I drew all manner of disaster. I had a feeling I would draw something fucked up, and I would not get my beer. And I really wanted that beer.

I pulled my sketch pad out my rucksack and grabbed the box of charcoal I took with me. Maybe I could draw something without having some sort of vision. Perhaps I could draw him dogs playing pool or something sweet.

I knew that was a lie as soon as I stared down at the blank page, and my vision blurred. I couldn't have fought it if I wanted to. I couldn't let go of the charcoal, and I couldn't stop my hand from drawing. All I knew was that something significant was either happening or coming, and I needed to put it on paper.

I furiously drew, even when my hand started cramping. I couldn't even make myself stop then. I couldn't stop until my vision finally cleared. I looked down. What the fuck did I draw this time? The bartender was leaning over the bar watching me.

"If that battle at the gate goes near as well as your drawing, I'll frame it and hang it in pride of place. Let me get you a beer."

I had to remember my drawings were always symbolism, and I didn't always understand them, because I certainly didn't understand this. I had drawn Aeron standing at the top of the gate with his sword out. The sword had flames coming from the blade, and Aeron had feathery wings spread out from his back, and every single person on the other side of the gate was dead.

I'd only seen a few of my paintings about the future, but none of them were in your face obvious. I could only guess Aeron had saved the day with some crazy idea. Even if he had saved California somehow, he would still hear it from me that he sent me away. I could have helped.

"I know you barter here, but do you place bets? I'll bet you another beer the man in that drawing will walk in this bar and tell us the wall is secure, and then I will punch him in the face."

"You must think highly of the man you're threatening to punch in the face if you drew him as an angel saving the city. Maybe save the punching for later. He was just trying to keep you safe."

He opened a bottle of beer and slid it across the bar. I gulped half the bottle down and slammed it back on the bar. I didn't take the time to savor it, even though I knew I was just getting the one.

"Tell you what. I like you, and this drawing is good. If your man gets back here with news the gate is secure, and we don't have to worry about the Brotherhood anymore, I'll give both of you a beer on the house."

"Deal. You got a name? Everyone calls me Speedy. We might be here a while."

"Jeff. You're welcome to stay here. Are you hungry? On the house since your man is off fighting the wall."

"He's not my man. He's just someone I'm traveling with."

"Does he know that? He went out of his way to get you out of danger."

"I could have fought. It's like he's saying he doesn't trust me to take care of myself."

"Or maybe he cares too much to risk your life in a hostile takeover."

"I guess."

I hadn't thought about it like that. I knew Aeron cared. I felt it when he used to hold me when we slept. We stopped doing that after my apartment because things just got weird. I missed it. I missed sleeping in his arms, and I hated that niggling feeling in my gut about Aeron.

He'd done nothing but protect me so far, and Miss Mabel trusted him. He took me back to my apartment, knowing those paintings were on my walls. He could have destroyed them, but he cleaned my apartment and left it the way it was for me.

Still, it didn't sit right with me that he didn't want Miss Mabel to tell me why I painted the things I did or that I had some weird gift when I put pen to paper. Sure, he helped after the cat was out of the bag, but if it were up to him, I'd still be in the dark. It was getting to the point that Aeron keeping secrets from me was starting to outweigh the feelings I was developing for him.

I would have thought a hostile takeover at the gate

would have taken a lot longer to quash, and Aeron would have to locate where Meremoth deposited me. Still, I had only just finished the sandwich Jeff gave me when he came strolling in without a drop of blood on him. His hair looked windblown in a sexy way, not like he fought a battle.

"We can leave now."

I grabbed the drawing off the bar and shoved it in his face.

"Care to explain this one?"

Aeron just shrugged.

"I had an idea, and we won."

Jeff popped open two beers and slid them across the bar.

"I promised Speedy beers for both of you if you came back and said the gate was secure. If it was your idea that kept the Brotherhood out, then I'd like to offer to feed you too. Are you hungry?"

"The sandwiches are excellent, and it will be our last hot meal for a while," I pointed out.

Aeron smacked his hand on the bar.

"Battles are best celebrated with ale, food, and wenches. I'll take a sandwich."

"Yeah, well, this wench is pissed off you sent me away."

"I had to, Ariel. You might not believe this, but I care about you more than the fact that to end all this, we need your blood. I'll protect you with my life, and if it means pissing you off, then so be it. As long as you don't get hurt, I will keep pissing you off."

Well, that was probably the sweetest thing anyone had ever said to me. Honestly, I couldn't remember the sweetest thing anyone could have possibly said to me, but for now, that was it. I guess I could forgive Aeron. I kept forgetting that it was my stupid mutant blood that caused all this, and I needed to stop being a dumbass and risking shit because my blood was somehow the key to stopping it.

"I'm sorry I got pissed, Aeron. I get it. Get the grilled cheese sandwich and tomato soup. It's fucking amazing. I get why you are protecting me, but no more secrets, okay?"

Jeff started preparing the food. He handed a plate and a bowl to Aeron, who dug in.

"Care you regale us with tales of battle, brother? What was your big idea that saved the gate?"

"Divide and conquer, my brother. There was more than one gang out there, so there was more than one gang leader. Pit them against each other, and they do the work for you."

Something didn't seem right about that. They seemed well organized, like they spent a lot of time trying to plan how to get through those gates. I heard someone say they made a shield wall out of car doors. What did I know? I'd never fought in any type of battle before. I slept through World War III. Maybe that worked.

People started spilling into the bar, and they all wanted to clap Aeron on the back and buy him a beer. He really was the hero at the wall. I would not question it. My drawing showed him saving the day, and everyone here was certainly confirming it.

Aeron had single-handedly saved California from a gang takeover while I sat on my ass, chatting with a bartender.

I would really have to contribute more.

THIRTY

Aeron didn't seem to have much of an ego as everyone at the bar seemed to want to kiss his ass. If anything, it seemed to embarrass him. It made me like him more, which made me want to bleach my lizard brain. Until Aeron told me the truth about everything, I couldn't feel that way about him. I could just tell he was keeping secrets.

We ended up having to stay at the border an additional day since the scuffle at the gate lost us several hours of daylight. Aeron didn't have an apartment right at the border, but someone at the gate let us crash at their place. He and Aeron bonded over killing gang members, and Aeron felt safe staying there.

We had to share a sofa bed, and it was super awkward. It was only a full, and Aeron and I were cramped. I could tell he was trying not to touch me because he didn't know how I would react, and I was trying not to fling myself across his chest and snuggle with him.

It was probably two in the morning, and both of us were awake.

"Ariel?" Aeron whispered.

"Yes?"

"Does it have to be like this?"

"You could have told me about the paintings."

"I didn't want to overwhelm you. A lot of shit has gone down while you were in a coma."

"Exactly! I'm already pretty fucking overwhelmed, and my memories are gone. Do you know what it feels like when you keep my past from me because you think I can't handle something?"

"Ariel, I'm sorry I didn't think you could handle painting the future on top of everything else."

"Aeron, you told me something in my blood managed to turn the majority of the world into the undead. Being able to paint the future is way less fucked up than that."

"I guess that's fair. You don't like it when I try to make decisions that I think will protect you."

"I can decide for myself what I'm ready to hear. I wouldn't ask if I didn't want to know."

"I'm sorry. I'll go against my instincts and try to stop doing that. Can I hold you while you sleep?"

I wanted him to. I could hear the vulnerability in his voice. I wanted to feel safe in his arms. I was feeling like some fucked up mutant. I could understand why Aeron was hesitant to tell me things, but that wasn't his decision to make. I wanted to snuggle up in his arms and forget for the night I was some kind of freak.

I wasn't ready for that, and I was still upset with Aeron. I had a feeling he knew exactly what kind of freak I was and why I could do those things, and he was keeping it from me.

"I'm not ready for that just yet, Aeron."

"Ariel, I vow this to you tonight. I will answer your

questions, but I promise you will have all the answers once you meet my entire team."

"Thanks, Aeron."

I rolled over and tried to get some sleep. My side of the sofa bed felt so cold and lonely.

THIRTY-ONE

We were up pretty early the next morning. For some reason, Aeron wanted me to close my eyes when we passed through the gates to leave California. He asked nicely, so I tried to do what he asked. Curiosity got the better of me, so I peeked. I immediately wished I hadn't.

There were dead bodies everywhere. There was a team of people lining up to throw them on a massive fire, but that wasn't what got my attention. After bashing in some Rage Head skulls, I was used to dead bodies. What the fuck had Aeron done at the gate? He said he turned the gangs against each other, but that was a lie. I saw one of the corpses before they threw it onto the fire. It was bloated and blackened like it had been dead for way longer than just one night.

"Are you going to tell me what actually happened at the gate, Aeron?"

"No, because you were a naughty girl and peeked when you weren't supposed to."

"Aeron, I thought we agreed on no secrets."

"Does it really matter, Ariel? Bad people died, and we stopped them from ruining a wonderful thing. You've seen your share of monsters since you woke up. I don't want you to think of me as one too because of how I stopped them."

"I don't think of you as a monster, Aeron."

"You aren't focusing on what's important, Ariel. Two more miles and we'll reach the border to Mexico. Leif has a lab in San Quintin, and the ride there will be rough. Some cities we will pass through are overrun with Rage Heads, and some people who are still alive will slit your throat over an unlabeled can of food. San Quintin put up walls like California and cleared out the Rage Heads. That's where the remaining military force is in Mexico, and if you think that scene at the gate in California was bad, it's worse in San Quintin."

"Then why are we going to Leif instead of Leif coming to us?"

"Because Leif has a top-notch research facility in San Quintin and armed guards to make sure he's not disturbed. Those are pretty scarce now."

I knew why I needed to meet them and do this, but I also had nightmares about the last time someone experimented on me.

"Aeron? Is Leif going to do the same things to me they did before?"

Aeron pulled me to his chest.

"Leif would never do that to you. None of us would ever hurt you."

"But why? It's my father doing all this, and it was my blood that caused all those people to mutate. Why did you approach me in that chatroom instead of just kidnapping me and taking what you needed?"

"Because we aren't the evil guys, Ariel. If you hadn't agreed to come, we would have tried harder, but even then, we wouldn't have just kidnapped you."

"Maybe you should have. Someone beat you to it."

"No, we should have just played it smarter when you left. Your father probably knew Leif and I were in Mexico and was watching border crossings."

"What's the deal with all of you and my father?"

"Stay alert, Ariel. That's the border to Mexico. Remember how it used to be a thing that the United States was so concerned about people crossing the border? Well, even though the United States took over Mexico during the war, Mexico doesn't want people coming in now either. Let me do the talking."

I remembered all the talk about some big, fancy border wall that would cost trillions of dollars and had so much controversy. There was undoubtedly a wall now. It looked like they crushed all the cars no one could use anymore and stacked them. There were military vehicles, school buses, and garbage trucks as far as I could see blocking the way in.

I couldn't see a single person, just stacked cars. Someone had turned the side of one of the garbage trucks into a door. A little slot slid open, and two eyes peered out.

"Well, look who finally came back. I hope it was worth it. One of the gangs tried eating some Rage Heads they killed because they were hungry. You can imagine how that turned out. We send these patrols out to cut down on the Rage Head population, then these assholes go and eat their flesh."

"It was worth it. I have what Leif needs."

"Looks to me like all you did was pick yourself up a girlfriend."

"Shut the fuck up, Martinez. Leif needs her."

"She doesn't look like any type of scientist to me. If Leif needed to get laid, he's got plenty of options here."

"Okay, that's offensive," I growled. "What does a scientist look like, anyway?"

"You look like the kind of girl who will beat my ass for checking you out and not a scientist."

"Oh, come on. A scientist would totally beat your ass for checking her out."

"She's right, Martinez. You're being a pig. Open the door."

"Oh, fine."

"And don't get grabby with my girl. She will totally kick your ass."

"You're no fun, Aeron."

The sliding panel on the side of the garbage truck slid open. Aeron backed Meremoth up, and we took a running start. Meremoth jumped inside, then skidded across the metal floor. Amazingly, he landed on all four hooves and didn't throw us when he landed on the ground on the other side.

"If the hot chick is important, do you want an escort to San Quintin?"

"The hot chick has a name and doesn't like to be called the hot chick," I snapped.

"Well, then be polite and introduce yourself if you don't want me giving you a nickname."

This guy right here.

"You can call me Speedy."

"Speedy doesn't sound like a scientist's name."

"You watch too many movies, Martinez. When has my

word never been good enough for you? We need her. What does the road to San Quintin look like since I've been gone?"

"Burned. There was some crossfire with a patrol and one of the gangs. They wasted good tequila throwing Molotov cocktails and started a huge fire. It raged out of control for several days before the rains finally came."

"So, my safe house is probably toast."

"And there will be stretches where you won't find a replacement place to crash either."

"I've got a tent. Is there a suitable area to camp?"

"Find the most burned-out area you can. Humans don't go there anymore because there is nothing to steal, and there's not a lot of Rage Heads because there are not a lot of humans to eat."

"Thanks, Martinez. We'll be on our way."

Was Aeron really going to ignore the fact that we got offered an escort? If people were burning shit down, I wouldn't mind more than the two of us to stop them from killing us. As soon as we were out of earshot of the piggish guard, I called Aeron on it.

"Is there any reason you didn't take him up on a guard for our journey?"

"Too many guns and egos."

"Oh, there's a raging ego, and it's sitting behind me on this horse. How are you and your fucking ego going to stop an entire gang when they throw Molotov cocktails at our tent?"

"The same way I dealt with the gangs at the gate. You heard Martinez. They have no reason to go back to a burned-out neighborhood. We'll find an area with good cover and pitch a tent for the night. I only have two sleeping bags, and you know how cold it gets at night. You can either freeze or stop being stubborn and let me keep you warm."

"So, you're back to being a dick to me?"

"I'm being logical. I won't deny that I want to hold you again, but the fact remains that the temperature drops at night, and we can't light a fire. It's cold cans and the snacks Mabel gave us for the road."

"Why didn't you tell me she was there when you said you were bringing me back to my apartment?"

"Because I knew seeing her face would help you remember better than me just mentioning it."

"I will be so mad if we manage to end this, and she's gone when I get back."

"Mabel will be waiting for you when you get back. I can guarantee you that."

"She has to be in her nineties now. Can I help it if I want to spend every minute with her now?"

"You will. We are just taking a detour to save the world."

We traveled through the street in silence. A few Rage Heads tried to bum rush us on the horse. I either got them with Smurfette or Aeron chopped their heads off with his sword. The Rage Heads here were a lot grosser than I'd seen in other states. These were burned to a crisp and stunk worse than the other.

Rage Heads kind of made these squishing and popping noises when their rotting bodies moved, but the burned ones kind of crackled. It was like you could hear their skin splitting open, and all manner of nastiness oozed from the cracks.

The fire had done a number on the landscape. It was pretty sad. It looked like this area might have escaped the bombs, but now everything was scorched and reduced to ash. This differed totally from the woods and ghost towns in Washington State and the community that had come together in California. This was people burning shit down for no reason.

The temperature was starting to drop, and the sky was going from orange to gray. That was usually a sign we would stop for the night. Aeron had this route planned down to a T. I didn't quite know what he was looking for until he pulled Meremoth up to a burned house with most of the brick structure still standing.

"We'll set up the tent in there. The walls will give us cover if there are any humans that come by, and it'll make it more difficult for the Rage Heads to get to us."

I could agree with that. Aeron left me to set up the tent like I'd been camping before. Honestly, I couldn't remember if I had or hadn't, but this tent didn't have an instruction manual, and I was probably not the best person for this job. Whatever he was doing, we probably needed it, so I struggled to get this fucking tent together.

I'd only managed to get half the tent up by the time Aeron had dismantled most of a burned car and strung up the pieces around the house. If anyone tried to come near our tent, we would hear them. Neat idea. If only I had contributed better with the tent. Aeron didn't say a fucking thing about it either. He just came over and started helping me.

We had the tent up in no time. Dinner was cold canned beans and homemade granola bars from Miss Mabel. God bless that woman because she was a mean cook, and if we weren't rationing food, I would have eaten all of those granola bars.

It was different sleeping in a tent. Not that I didn't mind roughing it. We were sleeping on top of rubble and burned flooring. It was just the drastic temperature difference between night and day now. It was so fucking hot during the day you sweat buckets. Most of the time, it was days before you could get a shower. As soon as the sky turned gray, it was like this switch got flipped to arctic.

We finished our dinner without talking much. We both knew what would happen next. I could either keep letting my lizard brain get in the way and freeze my ass off all night or get over my shit and share body heat with Aeron.

I was tired of this. He swore he would tell me everything when I met all of his team, and I believed him. Sure, he omitted the truth like what really happened at the gate, and he kept trying to decide what I was ready to hear, but at the rate I was having shit flung at me, it might eventually get to be too much. Maybe Aeron would answer one of my questions, and I would totally lose it. I mean, he'd told me some pretty fucked up shit so far. I needed to stop getting mad at him.

"Want to use one sleeping bag as a mattress and the other as a blanket?"

I only had to ask, and Aeron set to work, making it happen. There wasn't room for pillows in the saddlebags, so we used rolled up shirts, but this could work. My entire body was frigid cold, and that sleeping bag looked warm. The one he spread out on the tent floor gave a little padding, but it would do. I yanked the other sleeping bag up to my neck and tried to get warm. I felt Aeron climb in behind me, but he kept his distance because I just told him I wasn't ready for this.

I was sure I was giving the man whiplash with my mood swings. I was expecting some snarky comments back.

"Can you hold me?"

Aeron spooned my back and nuzzled my neck.

"I was hoping you would ask. I'll always try to get you whatever you ask for."

And he had. Except for answers to some of my questions. I didn't want to think about that. I just needed to accept that Aeron gave his word that I would eventually have all the answers. I turned in his arms and gazed into those silver eyes of his. Aeron had shaved his face with this massive pocket knife when we had water to spare, but right now, he had blond stubble on his chin. I caressed his cheek.

"I'm sorry. I'm being a brat. I know you're doing the best you can, it's just really frustrating that I can't remember. I remembered everything about Miss Mabel when I saw her face. I got bits and pieces in my apartment, but I still don't remember why I painted those paintings or why they made me agree to meet with you."

"You trusted Leif and me by then. You hadn't confided in us about what he did to you when you were a child, but we talked about everything else. Leif always says the first thing that pops into his head. He finally just told you that we knew who your father was and that he was up to something. It spooked you, and you disappeared for a week. You didn't come to the chatroom, and you wouldn't text or call. You called both of us on three-way a week later to say you were coming because you painted something confirming he was up to something big."

"And the sex painting in my bedroom?"

"I had to get embarrassed when Mabel presented that to me after she beat me with her broom. She—"

I interrupted him. I wanted to remember what we talked about so severely, and yes, I wanted to do this again ever since Aeron did it the first time. I tangled my hands in his silky hair and pulled him in for a kiss. Aeron let out a little growl and rolled me on my back. I dug my nails in his neck and wrapped my legs around his waist. Aeron was nibbling on my neck when we heard the jangle of hubcaps.

Aeron buried his face in my neck.

"To be continued," he whispered.

He placed his finger over my lips to be totally quiet. He didn't need to tell me. It could either be torched Rage Heads or humans wanting to slit our throats out there. That was when I heard it. They weren't even trying to be quiet. It was humans outside our tent.

Aeron grabbed his sword and went charging out of the tent. I could hear him trying to talk to them, telling them we didn't want any trouble. I didn't care what he would say later, I grabbed Smurfette and joined him.

There were five men wearing masks at the front of our tent. They didn't speak English, and I only spoke a little Spanish. I got the gist of what they were saying. They would let Aeron keep his tent and supplies if he gave them me to play with. That wasn't happening. I'd bash their brains in myself. It didn't look like they had any flaming tequila bottles to throw at us. They had machetes and knives.

Three of the men moved in on Aeron, and the other two tried to grab me. Bashing an unarmed Rage Head's brains in was easy, but fighting two men with machetes was a little complicated. It turned out one of them spoke English.

"Hello, sexy. Why don't you put that bat down? I'd hate to scar up that pretty face."

I didn't know the first thing about fighting someone

with a machete, but I knew I wasn't getting kidnapped and raped tonight. I swung hard at the man closest to me. I think I surprised him. He wasn't expecting me to fight back. Smurfette connected with his hand, and his machete when clattering away.

Now what? If I bashed his brains in, the other man with a machete could cut my fucking head off. I rather enjoyed having my head attached to my body. I held Smurfette up in a defensive position. The other guy with the machete was holding back, probably watching my fighting style. I needed to take the unarmed man out of the equation.

I swung Smurfette at his knees. I heard a sickening crack as his knee broke. He fell over howling. I'd deal with him in a minute. I still had my eyes on that second machete. This guy didn't speak a word of English, but I was pretty sure he put a curse on my first-born child. I know he called me a bitch.

"That's not very nice."

I decided to just go for it. He wasn't a big guy; he only had a big fucking knife. And that big fucking knife was scary. I decided to be scary too. I raised Smurfette above my head and just ran at him. I used the guy with the broken knee to launch myself in the air with my bat above my head.

The guy with the big scary knife cowered in fear as he tried to block me with his machete. I smashed the bat on his head and felt the machete slice my forearm. He fell over in a heap. I looked over, and Aeron had already beheaded the three men who came at him. I expected him to give me shit about not staying in the tent, but he didn't. He just winked at me.

"Not bad, Speedy. Finish them off so I can move the bodies. We need to get some sleep."

"You want to sleep after this?"

"You're bleeding," Aeron said, dashing over.

He drove his sword into the two men that attacked me and started checking my forearm.

"I will have to stitch this up. I've got a bottle of antibiotics. Go in the tent and put pressure on it while I move the bodies far away from us. We can use them as Rage Head bait. Hopefully, they'll be satisfied with these guys as their meal and leave us alone.

My forearm was throbbing, and five gang members wanted to trade me for camping supplies. I was about to try to sleep with bleeding corpses nearby for Rage Heads to eat.

I officially hated camping.

THIRTY-TWO

I really liked where things were headed before Aeron and I were so rudely interrupted. Even if I wasn't sitting here getting my arm stitched up in the dark and wondering how close those dead bodies were, we couldn't recapture that mood. Stitches fucking hurt too. I was trying to shine Aeron's flashlight on my arm while he tried not to mangle my arm further.

"Your first apocalypse battle scar. How does it feel?"

"Like I slammed my arm towards the end of a machete, and now you are sticking needle and thread through my arm."

"You've got a pretty extreme pain tolerance."

"Look at my arms. I wouldn't have sat and gotten all this inked on me if I didn't."

"Let me tie this off, and then I'm done. I'm almost out of ointment, but I've got some expired antibiotics for you to take. Leif will have what we need to keep this from getting infected when we get to San Quintin."

"And how did Leif end up with all the medical supplies in Mexico?"

Aeron cut the thread and started rubbing his last remaining ointment in my arm.

"It was just Leif and me at first. We weren't just sitting around in Mexico, plotting to get close to you. We were networking. Before they fell, we had the ear of the Mexican government, and the military is still on our side. We helped them during the war. We were looking for you and trying to stop your father, but we were fighting just like everyone else was. They know Leif can help end this, so they go out and get him what he needs. It's nice to have friends with good toys."

I just shrugged.

"I feel like all I'm contributing is my fucked up blood and drawings that might not make sense."

Aeron grabbed my shoulders and made me look him in the eye.

"Listen to me right now, Ariel. Your blood is not fucked up. Nothing about you is fucked up. You are exactly as you need to be. Stop focusing on how Isaiah polluted it for evil purposes and think about the fact that Leif will use it to stop this."

"There's a reason I'm at the center of this, isn't there? And you won't tell me until your entire team is with you."

"Ariel, if you think shit is terrible now, it will only get worse. If you are focusing on the evil things that your father did with your blood instead of the marvelous things Leif can do with it, then you will need a support system when you get the full picture. *That's* why I want my team there before I tell you everything.

"We are all different. We can comfort you in distinct ways. You might need something I can't give, as much as that kills me. We aren't just roping you into this because of who you are and what your blood can do. Even after

Leif gets your blood and figures out what to do with it, it's our job to get you back to California, safe and sound. The only reason you are coming to Washington with us is so we can keep you safe while we stop your father. Then, I will bring you back to Mabel."

"And then?" I demanded.

What was with his whole snuggling and stealing kisses? Why did he tell me we couldn't have sex until I remembered him if he was just babysitting me until he could dump me back at home? Was this some plot to fuck with my head so I wouldn't leave?

Aeron just grinned at me.

"Well, I was hoping that painting might come true like the rest of your paintings do."

I punched Aeron in the arm. He was back to being a dick, but I guess I could admit I liked it when he did.

"So, what? We have an orgy in the Oval Office, and you dump me back at home, then we all go our separate ways?"

Aeron nipped at the tip of my nose.

"No, I'm saying after the orgy, you will want to keep us and will have to get a bigger apartment."

"Go to bed, Aeron."

I didn't even know his team. I was developing pretty strong feelings for Aeron, but I also knew I had pretty strong opinions on cheating.

I was *not* having an orgy in the Oval Office. I didn't care what that painting said. I was probably just high when I painted it.

THIRTY-THREE

We actually did it. We managed to travel through a bombed-out landscape with mutated corpses who wanted to eat us with just a sword, a blue baseball bat, and a crazy horse. We didn't do it alone. Gabriel's Haven helped, and so did the entire state of California. That right there told me the world was still worth saving. I'd been scared, hungry, and dirty, but the worse thing that happened to me was a long line of stitches in my arm.

Still, I was nervous. Did I have some sort of online relationship with Leif like I did with Aeron? I couldn't remember anything about my chats with Leif. If he had been looking for me as hard as Aeron and we had something going, he would be excited to see me. And I would crush him by not remembering a single thing about it.

It was easy remembering with Miss Mabel. All I had to do was see that kind, beautiful, lined face, and I just remembered. I didn't have that with Aeron or Leif. I'd never met them in person. The only way I remembered things with Aeron was when he told me something, and it triggered a memory. I was pretty sure that kiss that unlocked some of my memories was our first kiss, but I couldn't even make logical sense of how I remembered things.

As much as I wanted to chit chat when we rode before, I just wanted silence right now. I wanted to be alone with my thoughts. When they were driving needles into my skin and taking my blood, they did everything they could to terrorize me. There were always flashing lights and had recordings of screaming playing. They couldn't even hear my tiny screams because they were playing it so loudly.

I just knew they weren't doing that because they enjoyed torturing children. There was a purpose. Wouldn't the same thing need to happen to make a cure? I didn't know the first thing about the science behind any of this.

I noticed the landscape started changing the further we got past the burned zone and closer to San Quintin. San Quintin didn't just set up a wall around the city. They'd booby-trapped everything within the vicinity.

I saw some same wood traps with sharp spikes. I also noticed Meremoth wasn't walking straight. He was walking like a drunk horse.

"Aeron, I know you've got a weird horse, but what is he doing?"

"They covered the pits. They've got deep pits dug all over the place to trap Rage Heads, murderers, and thieves. That was my idea. The big wooden pikes were Leif's design."

"But we saw them in Washington State."

"Because I taught this to the good people. Some wicked people saw and built their own. Armed soldiers will meet us when we pass that crumbled statue. Don't worry. They are on our side."

"Are they going to Lady Scientist me like your friend Martinez?"

"He's an ass, but I'd trust him at my back in battle. Don't make any sudden moves when we get close to that statue. They will shoot to kill if they think you are a threat."

I had a healthy appreciation for not getting shot to death, so I tried to lay Smurfette across Meremoth, where she was less visible. I was holding my breath when we got to that statue. All I could see was a pair of legs. The rest of the statue was in rubble by the base.

Don't ask me where they came from. They just sort of appeared out of nowhere, but ten soldiers surrounded us with guns pointed right at my chest.

"State your business!"

"I need to get this woman to Leif. She's part of our team."

This young kid, who couldn't have been more than sixteen and seemed pretty trigger happy, raised his gun.

"Who are you, and how do you know Leif?"

"Who the fuck are you that you don't know me, Sparky?"

A man stepped forward and lowered the kid's gun for him.

"It's fine, Javier. Aeron fought in the war, and he's on Leif's team. You just don't remember because you hadn't joined up before he left."

"Sorry," the kid grumble.

"This girl is why you've been gone so long?"

"She's the missing piece, so you need to protect her

with your life, and if I find you disrespecting her, I'll throw you through a wall."

One man snapped to attention. He was all soldier.

"Men, we have a mission. Escort the princess to the castle and save the kingdom."

Okay, and apparently a video game geek, but I could work with that. It was like this fucking military parade as they led us safely through all their booby traps. We finally got to the fence, and they took it just as seriously as California did. It was made of sheet metal and barbed wire, but San Quintin took it a step further. There were pikes at the top of the fence, and they had stuck heads on them. Some of them were Rage Heads based on the red eyes that were getting a white film over them, but some of them looked human.

"Do we want to go in there, Aeron? They've got human heads on pikes!"

"Your head only goes up there if they are making an example of you. All those human heads belong to murderers, cannibals, and rapists."

Was that supposed to make it less gross? If I got inside these walls and people were wearing body parts as trophies, I'm not sure I could make myself stay. What if Leif ended up this total psycho?

"Calm down, Ariel. We are safe here. None of these men will hurt you, and you know Leif."

"I don't remember a fucking thing about Leif!"

"But, you might when you meet him."

Our escorts led us all the way to a pristine white building that didn't look like it had been through a war. Aeron helped me off Meremoth and unloaded the saddlebags.

There was either solar power, or they got the power

grid working here too because the front doors slid open, and air conditioning hit me right in the face. The sun was still out, and I was sweaty and nasty. I had a layer of soot all over my face from running through all that burned territory—way to make an excellent first impression.

I wanted to kiss Aeron when he led me down to an area with group showers. I just wanted to get clean, but this was apparently to decontaminate ourselves before we went further inside. I planned on decontaminating myself under this hot water and a fresh bar of soap until someone made me get out. I had exactly one pair of clean underwear left, and I couldn't wait to slip it on.

I was enjoying my shower so much, I wasn't even paying attention to the hot, wet naked guy next to me. Aeron was watching me, though.

"As much as I'm enjoying watching you play in the water, we do need to go meet Leif."

I turned and took in Aeron in all his wet, naked glory. My mouth went dry. Fuck, did he ever look beautiful. And his cock was hard and standing right at attention from watching me shower. What I wouldn't give for some shower sex right about now. One day, Aeron and I would get our moment, and I had a feeling it would be epic.

"Little Aeron doesn't look like he wants to go meet Leif."

"Are you calling my junk little, Speedy?"

"No, it looks like a fucking baby arm, but it's pointed right at me."

"The apocalypse is a huge cockblock, Ariel. We can either sneak away and have sex, or you can go meet Leif and find out some answers you've been asking me."

Why couldn't we do both?

THIRTY-FOUR

I decided not to go straight for the cock option, even if I was a little mad about it. If I remembered right, I was twenty-six when I got kidnapped, and I slept a long time. I was too old to be shirking responsibility to get laid. I was too old to be having sex with Aeron because I was nervous about meeting with Leif. Plus, when Aeron and I took that step, I wanted it to be special.

As soon as we stepped out of the bathroom, someone showed up to take all our dirty clothes. Were they going to wash them for us? How sweet. Washing your clothes during the apocalypse was pretty complicated, and if you got rank while wearing them, sometimes they were still rank when you put them back on after washing them. I'm still not talking about the few pairs of panties I had.

Aeron grabbed my hand and walked me over to an elevator. There was no up button, just a pad. Aeron's fingerprint was what opened the door. I wasn't sure how I felt about getting into an elevator at the end of the world, but when I mentioned that to Aeron, he said it was the only way to the lab.

We went down instead of up. We went way down. Was this lab underground? When the doors opened, I wasn't prepared for what I saw. There was lab equipment, sure, but there was also satellite tracking, computers, and it looked like someone was diagraming something on the wall.

I couldn't see anyone in the lab. Where was the mysterious Leif?

"Speedy!" I heard someone yell.

Someone came flying at me and practically tackled me with a hug. This had to be Leif. He was just as huge as Aeron with black hair and black eyes. He had a ring through his septum and another through his eyebrow. Leif spun me around and set me down.

I had no idea what he was doing when he fell on his knees in front of me. He grabbed my hand and kissed my knuckles.

"Milady, the Horseman of Pestilence is at your service."

"Excuse me?"

Aeron smacked Leif on the back of the head.

"I haven't told her about that yet. There's still a lot she doesn't remember."

He didn't need to tell me. I'd known this entire time, and I'd denied it to myself. The horses I kept painting, Meremoth's behavior, the blackened corpses at the gate. I knew, and I kept denying it because I didn't want it to be true.

I had been traveling with and had fallen in love with the Horseman of Death.

Afterword

I hope you enjoyed Book 1 of End of Days. This is a slow burn series and we will meet a new harem member in each book. In the next book, which will be out as soon as I finish Monster Whisperer, things will heat up between Aeron and Ariel, secrets will be reveals, and we'll get to know all about the dark, mysterious Leif.